THE MASKED MARKSMAN:
DEATH TAKES AN ENCORE
AND OTHER STORIES

THE MASKED MARKSMAN

DEATH TAKES
AN ENCORE
AND OTHER STORIES

By Emile C. Tepperman

POPULAR PUBLICATIONS • 2023

PUBLISHING HISTORY

"Amateur Night—for Killers" originally appeared in the September, 1934 (Vol. 3, No. 4) issue of *The Spider* magazine. "Cue for a Corpse" originally appeared in the October, 1934 (Vol. 4, No. 1) issue of *The Spider* magazine. "The Death Juggler" originally appeared in the November, 1934 (Vol. 4, No. 2) issue of *The Spider* magazine. "Death's Spotlight" originally appeared in the February, 1935 (Vol. 5, No. 1) issue of *The Spider* magazine. "Billed for Death!" originally appeared in the March, 1935 (Vol. 5, No. 2) issue of *The Spider* magazine. "Death's Booking Agent" originally appeared in the April, 1935 (Vol. 5, No. 3) issue of *The Spider* magazine. "Death Takes an Encore" originally appeared in the May, 1935 (Vol. 5, No. 4) issue of *The Spider* magazine. "Murder in the Spotlight" originally appeared in the June, 1935 (Vol. 6, No. 1) issue of *The Spider* magazine. Copyright 2023 by Argosy Communications, Inc. All rights reserved.

Visit POPULARPUBLICATIONS.com for more books like this.

AMATEUR NIGHT—FOR KILLERS

T HE TRAIN pulled into Newbold City at nine in the morning. Ed Race walked out of the station with only a small overnight bag. The paraphernalia for his vaudeville act had gone ahead to the Newbold Theater, and his own personal luggage, including the six precious revolvers that he cleaned lovingly every single day, were probably already at the Coulter Hotel.

The overnight bag did not contain clothes. It held certain objects which he found advisable always to carry with him ever since he had become a private detective as a side line.

An expensive imported limousine awaited him outside the main entrance of the theater. A square-jawed, powerfully-built chauffeur touched his cap with deference. "Mr. Race, sir? Judge Hepley sent his car for you. I'll take you right over."

Ed Race eyed the chauffeur keenly. "That's funny. I thought the judge was going to keep my coming a secret from everyone."

The chauffeur shrugged. "The judge must have confidence in me, sir." He held the door open respectfully.

Ed cast a glance up the main street of the thriving little Pennsylvania city. He knew from the judge's letter that he ought to be extremely careful. Yet it seemed quite in character that Judge Hepley should send a car for him. He stepped into the limousine, and the door closed behind him.

1

Immediately, he knew he had been trapped! His swift glance showed him that there were no handles to open the closed windows, none on the inside to open the doors.

He had his gun out in an instant, raised the butt to shatter the window. There was a click, and steel shutters slid up to cover the glass, plunging the interior of the car in blackness. The limousine leaped away from the curb. There was the sound of smoothly meshing gears, and the car settled down to a swift, steady pace.

Kidnapped! Before he had a chance to get into this game of death that was being played in Newbold City, he had been snatched away. Judge Hepley had warned him in the letter that the people he was going to oppose were ruthless—swiftly efficient. Here was a sample.

Ed Race smiled ruefully. He should have known better. He was no novice. He held a license as a private detective in a half-dozen states, but he preferred to tour the country in a vaudeville circuit, doing a juggling act with forty-five caliber revolvers. The startling part of his number came when he juggled three guns at one time. As each gun came down into his hand he shot out the flame of a candle thirty feet across the stage. He was one vaudeville headliner that had no imitators!

He felt the speed of the car increasing, and he set to work. His fingers moved nimbly, opening the overnight bag. From among its contents he selected a midget acetylene torch, made by a clever machinist to his own specifications. In a moment he had donned a pair of goggles. He pressed the little spring-catch of the torch, and directed the sizzling, blue-white flame at a spot in the right hand door just above the lock. He traced a circle around

the spot, watched the bullet-proof metal burn away under the flame. When the circle was completed, he struck it hard with the butt of his gun, and a round piece about twelve inches in diameter fell away. The door, minus its lock, was swung open by the rush of the wind as the swiftly moving vehicle careened along.

Ed replaced the torch and goggles, and closed the bag. Then he swung out on the running board. They were speeding through a mixed residential and shopping section of the city, and he could see a policeman directing traffic at the next crossing.

He edged along the running board till he was beside the driver's seat, and clung tightly to the door-frame with his left hand. With his right, he shoved his gun into the chauffeur's ribs below the armpit, and shouted above the wind, "Pull up, guy!"

The chauffeur turned a startled face, looked quickly ahead,

watching the road. He grinned, showing discolored molars. "Go ahead and shoot, Race. Can you figure what'll happen to you if we crash—standing on the running board like that?"

They were approaching the intersection. Ed pocketed his gun, reached into the car, and yanked on the emergency! The car shrieked to a stop, skidding to a stop within a foot of the traffic officer.

Ed stepped from the running board, took out his gun. "Get out!" he rapped.

The chauffeur obeyed, with a quirked smile. He didn't seem especially perturbed. The traffic cop ran around the front of the car, tugging his gun out. "What the hell do you call this?" he shouted.

Ed showed his shield. "Take a look at the car. I had to cut my way out of it. I want to hold this guy for kidnapping."

The cop eyed the shield, grunted. "Kidnapping, huh? Hot stuff!" Then his eye lit on the chauffeur, and he gasped, saluted mechanically. "Lieutenant Barney!—I didn't recognize you."

The chauffeur frowned, trying to catch the cop's eye. A small crowd was gathering. Ed Race tensed. He jerked a thumb at the chauffeur, asked the cop, "Did I hear you call him *Lieutenant?*" THE COP shuffled. "Well—"

"Wait a minute," said the chauffeur. "Let's go where we can talk this over. No sense in havin' the crowd listen in. Pile in the car and we'll drive around the corner. You, too, Bauer, to make Mr. Race feel safe."

"Suits me," said Ed.

The traffic officer bellowed the crowd away, and the three of them got into the car. Barney took the wheel. Ed and the officer sat in the rear. The cop gaped at the hole in the door.

"No tricks," Ed warned. "Law or no law, I hate being snatched!"

Barney drove down three blocks, and parked before an open lot.

"All right," Ed suggested. "Now, what's it all about?"

"It's all about this!" Barney snarled. He twisted around to face them, stuck the ugly snout of an automatic over the back of the seat, pointing it squarely at Ed.

Ed's gun was hanging negligently between his knees. He sat still. Barney kept his eyes on Ed, but spoke to the cop. "Bauer, this guy has a reputation, but he's really dumb. Look how he played into my hands. Take him downtown and charge him with assault with a deadly weapon. That ought to hold him till we're through with our little business."

Bauer said, doubtfully, "Whose business, Lieutenant?"

Ed Race spoke quietly. "Look, Bauer, your friend Mr. Barney seems to be a police-lieutenant in disguise. But it looks to me like he's a crook. Are you going to back his play?"

Bauer appeared uncertain of his ground. "I don't know about this, Lieutenant. After all—"

"Forget it, Bauer," Barney snapped. "This is the Chief's business. You can take this mugg downtown, or get broke!"

Bauer sighed. "Well, if it's the Chief's business—" He reluctantly took out his handcuffs. "Hand over your gun, you!" he growled at Ed.

Ed gingerly lifted the gun from between his knees, holding it by the barrel in his left hand. He extended it to Bauer, butt first. Bauer reached for it. Then Ed acted with the lightning speed for which he was famous on the stage. Apparently by accident, the gun dropped from his fingers. His right hand swooped out faster than the eye could follow, and caught the gun in midair. At the same time, his left hand reached up, gripped Bauer by the back of the neck in powerful fingers, and yanked mightily!

Bauer's body was pulled to the side, fell into Ed's arms. Barney cursed. He couldn't shoot now without hitting Bauer. The patrolman's face went white under Ed's punishing grip on his neck.

Ed's gun was trained on Barney. He said silkily, "If you will kindly put your gun down, Lieutenant Barney, or whatever your name is, and get to hell out of this car, I will appreciate it. I like your company, but I have places to go."

Barney growled, "This won't get you anywhere, Race. You're up against a big thing, here. If I don't get you, someone else will. Take my advice. Leave this town and forget about the Judge. It might even pay you to pass up your act at the theater tonight."

"Thanking you for your advice, I am yours very truly," Ed replied. "Now, get!"

Barney said, "O. K. But remember, I warned you." He let his gun drop to the floor and stepped out of the car.

"Now pull your friend out," Ed directed. Bauer was semi-conscious from the wicked grip at the nape of his neck. It was a deadly grip—one that could kill a man if used properly. Barney hauled the man out, supported him on the sidewalk, glaring at Ed the while.

Ed slipped into the driver's seat, shifted into gear and stepped on the gas pedal. He grinned into Barney's wrathful face. "I'm sure you won't mind my borrowing this bus," he sang out.

He took a right turn at the next corner, then zig-zagged in and out of a half-dozen streets, to make sure he shook off all pursuit. He estimated it would be five minutes before an alarm could get out. Well within that limit, with a minute to go, he abandoned the car. He took his little bag, boarded a passing trolley. When the trolley got to a busier section of the city, he got off, flagged a cab, and said, "15 Emmons Street. No objection if you snap it up."

JUDGE SUMNER HELPEY'S home on Emmons Street was a modest, refined-looking two-story frame building. It was one of a row of better than average houses on the tree-lined street. Each had a plot of carefully-trimmed lawn in front, and a garage in the rear.

Ed said to the chauffeur, "Here's an extra dollar. Take that bag down to the Coulter Hotel, and leave it at the desk for Mr. Race."

"It's a pleasure, boss," said the cabby. "That's an easy buck, what I call."

When the cab left, Race walked up the narrow path, took the three porch steps in a leap, and pushed the button. He heard a bell jangle inside. As if his ring had been a signal of some sort, a gun was suddenly discharged within the house. The report reverberated through the building.

Ed turned the knob, and pushed. The door opened at his touch, and he tore into the hallway. There was scant light here, except for some stray beams that crept in through the entrance.

To the left was an open doorway, leading to a library. Ed Race stepped through it. A portly, white-haired man sagged in the chair before the massive oak table. His head hung over the back of the chair at an unnatural angle. He was dead. He had been shot in the heart.

Ed sprang to the open window which looked on the driveway alongside the house. A man in a gray topcoat was sprinting around the end of the garage at the rear. Ed pulled his gun and fired in a single motion, too swift for the eye to follow. The man in the topcoat disappeared behind the garage, but Ed knew he had hit him. He knew just where. All he had been able to see at the moment of firing had been the right shoulder, and his slug had spanged there.

Ed vaulted the window sill, hit the cement driveway on a run. His long legs ate up the distance to the garage. His quarry had sped through the driveway of the house which backed on Judge Hepley's. He was just turning into the other street. Ed had no time for another shot. He sped through the driveway and just as he got out on the other street, saw a coupé pull away from the curb with a roaring motor. Ed raised his gun, aimed at the tires, but before he could shoot, his arm was grabbed from behind and someone hit him a terrific whack on the side of the head.

His head spun. He sagged, would have fallen, except that rough arms that caught him. Someone shouted in his ear, "What you think this is, a shootin' gallery?"

It was a uniformed policeman. Ed was weak but he kept his wits. As if by magic, his gun disappeared into one of his pockets. He rested heavily in the policeman's arms, giving his head time to clear.

Curious people were coming out of the houses along the street; a small crowd was gathering. Ed heard the cop say, "My club grazed the side of his head. He'll be all right in a minute."

Ed grunted and began to straighten up. He looked at the policeman. "So you're a cop, huh?" he growled. "Well, you did a fine job! Judge Sumner Hepley has just been murdered back there in his house! And you sock me just when I've got the killer in the bag! You ought to get a medal—from the murderer!"

"You don't say so!" the cop snarled. "Judge Hepley has just been killed, and you're trying to catch the murderer! Well, well! You couldn't be the killer, could you? Let's go back there and see what it's all about."

They started back through the driveway, the cop keeping a grip on Ed's arm. He called out to the bystanders, "Call Headquarters, one of you. Say there's been a murder, and that I got the guy. Me, Patrolman Joe Franz, Fourteenth Precinct."

JUDGE HEPLEY'S house was already in a state of turmoil. Some of the neighbors had probably 'phoned about the shot, for a police radio-car stood before the door. Two policemen from the car were in the library.

A middle aged woman in a house dress and dusting cap was talking to them. As Patrolman Franz pushed Ed Race in before him, one of the two cops from the radio-car was barking at the woman, "Who are you? What's happened here?"

The woman could not take here eyes off the Judge's body. "Lord help us," she muttered. "The poor Judge!"

The cop shook her arm roughly. "Come on, speak up I What's your name?"

She looked up at him as if suddenly aware of his presence. "Mrs. Davis is my name," she snapped. "I'm the housekeeper." She looked at the body again. "Poor Judge, he had nobody to take care of him but me."

"Where were you when this happened?" the man in uniform rasped.

"Upstairs. I heard a shot and came down. I rushed in here and there was the poor Judge lying all bloody, and someone was climbing out of the window."

Just then she caught sight of Ed Race. Her eyes snapped. She lifted a gnarled hand and pointed a bony, accusing finger at Ed. "That's him!" she shrieked. "That's who I saw climbing out the window! He done it! He done it!" She shook her finger under Ed's nose. "You murdered him! What did the poor Judge ever do to you? Why did you kill him?"

"My dear Mrs. Davis," Ed smiled at her with his lips, though his eyes were grim. "Don't judge by appearances. Maybe if I tell you my name, it will mean something to you. I am Ed Race."

The woman uttered a strangled cry and put her fist to her mouth. Her eyes were wide with consternation. "What have I done!" she moaned. "The man who was to save my son! You're the one the Judge sent for!"

Just then the outer door opened. Patrolman Franz said, "That will be someone from headquarters."

Ed looked to the doorway and a slow grin spread over his face, for the man who entered was Lieutenant Barney, minus his chauffeur's uniform. He was dressed in plain clothes, and was chewing a toothpick. Barney's eyes swept the room, taking in the body of Judge Hepley, flicking past Ed Race with no hint of recognition. "All right, boys," he said easily, "I'll take charge."

He walked to within a foot of Ed, asked, "This the murderer?"

Patrolman Franz nodded. "I caught him on Union Street. He was running away with a gun in his hand, so I pasted him one."

"Well, don't just stand there!" Barney snapped. "Take out your gun and cover him! What do you think this is? A party?"

Franz complied, poking his gun into Ed's back.

Barney said, "What's your name? Remember anything you say may be used against you!"

"My dear Barney," said Ed, "your memory is getting bad. Less than a half-hour ago we were having a pleasant talk in your big car. And now you don't know me!"

The other regarded him coolly. "You're crazy, I never saw you before in my life. But just in case you feel funny, maybe this'll sober you!" His fist came up in a short swing and caught Ed in the mouth. The blow was intended to loosen a couple of teeth, but Ed swung his head back easily and got nothing more than a cut lip.

One of the other cops jumped in and grabbed hold of Ed's other hand. The private detective strained forward, but Franz and the other cop held on to him grimly. Ed felt a trickle of blood on his chin. His eyes blazed bright at Barney.

Barney turned away with a grin, looked at Mrs. Davis. "Who's this?" he demanded.

"The Judge's housekeeper," Franz told him. "She saw this guy climb out of the window right after the shot was fired."

"That right?" Barney asked her.

Mrs. Davis was keeping herself calm with an effort. She looked Ed Race over closely. "On second thought," she said, "I guess maybe he isn't the man. Yes, I must have been mistaken. The one I saw didn't resemble this gentleman at all."

FRANZ SPAT disgustedly. "Hell," he exclaimed, "I just heard her identify him with my own ears. She's just covering him up now."

Barney shrugged. "I know her. It's her brat, Frank Davis, that's coming up for sentence tomorrow for the Wilson murder. Race is the guy they were getting to dig up new evidence to save the kid. It's only natural for her to try to shield him, but she'll change her tune downtown. We'll hold her as a material witness. By and by she'll get disgusted with that, and talk our way."

Ed licked the blood from his lips, said, "You seem to know a lot about things you're not supposed to know. I bet you have a dictograph planted somewhere in this house."

Barney grinned. "You'll find out we're not so dumb in this town—when you hang for murder yourself! Maybe we can fix it so you'll swing with this kid Frank Davis." Then to Franz, "Did you frisk him?"

"We didn't get a chance to."

"Well, do it! No, wait a minute! I'll do it myself."

He ripped open Ed's coat, dug into the breast pocket His hand came out with a square envelope. It was addressed to Edward Race. Barney examined the angular handwriting, made sure that the letter was still inside the envelope, and then started to put it in his own pocket.

"I want a receipt for that letter!" Ed Race rapped.

Barney's eyes narrowed, "I'll give you a receipt, all right!" He raised his hand, fist clenched, for a back-handed swing at Ed's face, but he never completed the blow—Franz whispered, "Cheese, Lieutenant! The inspector's here!"

Barney's eyes smoldered. He turned slowly toward the newcomer in the doorway. This man was dressed in plain clothes; he had a quiet air of authority. His clear blue eyes narrowed in disapproval. "How many times have I told you," he demanded of the sullen lieutenant, "that I want no third-degree stuff in my squad. Maybe you have a lot of drag higher up, Barney, but, by God, while I'm inspector, you'll take orders from me! Is that clear?"

"I'm sorry, Inspector Mason," Barney murmured with an undertone of resentment in his voice. "I lost my temper. This prisoner was caught practically in the act of murder—there's Judge Hepley's body, still warm—and the woman identified him, then changed her mind!"

Inspector Mason strode into the room. "What's your name?" he asked Ed.

"Edward Race. I'm known as an actor."

Mason started. His mouth twitched, but he showed no other sign of excitement. "Clear the room!" he ordered curtly.

Franz and the other cop grudgingly released their grip on Ed, went out. Barney planted himself in front of his superior. "But listen, Inspector! This guy is a murderer! You ain't goin' to leave yourself alone in a room with him!"

"I said, clear the room!"

Barney shrugged and went out. The corpse of the murdered man seemed to watch his exit out of sardonically staring eyes. Mason put his hand on Mrs. Davis's shoulder. "You stay!" he said.

When the door closed behind Barney, Mrs. Davis burst out excitedly. "That's Mr. Race, Inspector, the man the Judge said was our only hope for saving my boy Frankie from hanging."

Mason nodded somberly. He extended his hand to Ed. "I know all about you. The Judge confided in me that you were going to play this town and he was going to ask you to help. I know, of course, that you did not kill the Judge. It's some ghastly frame-up of Commissioner Snead's. Barney is in on it, as usual, of course. He does Snead's dirty work. He takes his orders direct from the Commissioner and disregards me entirely. It looks as if you are in bad spot."

ED TOOK out a pack of cigarettes and offered it to Mason. When the Inspector refused, he lit one himself, drawled through a cloud of smoke, "Where does this Commissioner Snead fit into the picture?"

"He fits, all right," Mason said. "And it's a nasty picture. Valentine Snead and his elephant of a son, Marvin Snead. Valentine used to be a ward-heeler, a petty politician, a go-between for the gangsters and the political clique that ran the town. Last year he got himself appointed Chief of Police. Anybody he doesn't like gets the works—like Judge Hepley, here. The judge has been fighting him and the administration for a long time. There are just a few of us on the force who have been rooting for the judge. Recently, it was hinted to me that I ought to retire, but, by God, I'm hanging on."

"Nice set-up," Ed grunted. He picked up his gun from the table where Franz had put it, sheathed it in the holster under his left arm-pit.

Mason watched him dejectedly. "How the devil did you get into this mess?" he asked.

"I suppose you know," Ed told him, "that the Judge wrote asking me to pay him a visit the minute I got into town. He wanted to interest me in the case of Mrs. Davis's son. He said Frankie had been convicted of the murder of Jack Wilson, a gambler, and that he was coming up for sentence tomorrow. But he was morally certain the boy was not guilty. He also said he had dug up certain information that would help me to unearth the real murderer."

Mason nodded gloomily. "So they got him before he could tell you anything. But how come this frame-up?"

Ed told him everything that had happened. A harried expression grew on Mason's face during the accounting. He shook his head hopelessly. "It's just like the Wilson murder. Frankie Davis is the goat there; they'll try to make you the goat here." He suddenly looked old. "I don't know what to do."

Ed Race grinned confidently. "Let me handle this, Inspector. These birds are right up my alley. Just give me the lay of the land! You say Snead and his son are running this business. Now, where would I find Snead?"

"He would be at Headquarters," Mason told him wearily

"Go up Emmons to State Street, then left till you hit the City Hall. Police Headquarters is across the street. You can't miss it. Of course, I'll release you now for lack of evidence—but what can you do alone? The minute I try to work with you, Snead will relieve me of duty—"

He stopped in the middle of the sentence. The door was shoved open and Lieutenant Barney strode in, grinning broadly. He had heard Mason's last words. "You're a prophet, Inspector," he said, pointing to the telephone on the table before the Judge's body. "There's a call coming in right now."

As confirmation of his statement, the 'phone burst into a jangle, weirdly disrespectful of Judge Hepley's stiffening body.

Mrs. Davis answered. "It's for you, Inspector."

Mason picked it up, said, "Hello! Yes, Commissioner." He listened a while, replaced the receiver, a beaten look on his face. "That was Commissioner Valentine Snead," he announced. "I have been ordered to deliver a lecture at the Police School this morning. I'm to turn the investigation of this case over to Lieutenant Barney."

Barney said, "Sorry, Inspector," as if he didn't mean it.

Mason said nothing more. He went out with his shoulders sagging.

Barney called after him. "Tell the fingerprint men and photographers to come in, will you, Inspector?"

He turned to Ed Race, with a nasty smile, but the smile faded and his mouth opened in astonishment, for Ed had his automatic out and was pointing it negligently at Barney. Mrs. Davis stared wide-eyed, speechless.

ED STEPPED over to Barney, took the gun out of the lieutenant's holster, and flipped it into a corner. Then he pocketed his own gun. He touched his split lip and grinned wickedly at the officer. "All right, you big stiff," he breathed, "I owe you this one!" His right fist flashed up in a swift, short arc. There was a terrific thud, followed by a crack. Barney's jaw jerked to an unnatural angle. He was lifted from his feet and catapulted against the wall. Ed massaged the knuckles of his hand. He winked at Mrs. Davis.

"Good bye, lady," he said. "Don't worry about Frankie." He patted her shoulder. "When the boys outside come in, give them my love." He swung his legs over the window-sill and dropped to the driveway. He headed back past the garage, through the driveway in the rear, and came out on Union Street again. He walked rapidly away, dabbing a handkerchief at his cut lip.

Two blocks away, he flagged a cab, said, "Coulter Hotel."

The Coulter was only a block from City Hall. At the desk he said to the clerk, "You got a bag for me? My name's Race."

"Yes, Mr. Race," the clerk answered. He handed the little bag over the counter. "Your baggage arrived this morning, sir. You have room fourteen, on the second floor. Here's the key." He eyed Ed queerly.

Ed took the key, started to go, then turned back. "Anything wrong?" he demanded.

The clerk coughed behind his hand, looked uncomfortable. "Well, I guess you ought to know this. There was a detective here from headquarters right after your baggage came this morning. He was up in your room for a little while, and then left."

Ed said, "Yeah. That's something I really ought to know." He took some bills out of his pocket.

The clerk saw the bills, looked around furtively, then leaned over the counter and whispered, "Here's something else—there's somebody up in your room right now. Commissioner Snead himself! I saw him come in a while ago, and go in the manager's office. The manager rang for me and told me to bring a pass key. When I entered with it, I heard the manager say to Snead, 'It's room fourteen. I don't like it, but if you say it's okay—' Then they stopped talking when they saw me."

"How long ago was this?" Ed asked.

"Less than five minutes ago. I guess he's still up there."

Ed crumpled a twenty-dollar bill in the palm of his hand, passed it over the counter. "Thanks," he said.

The clerk's eye caught the figure "20" on the bill. "Thank *you*, sir!" he breathed fervently.

Ed left the bag at the desk and sprinted across the lobby. He disregarded the elevator, took the staircase. On the second floor he walked carefully down the corridor, and tried the door of his room. It was locked. Somebody within growled, "Who's that?"

"Telegram for Mr. Race," Ed piped, making his voice shrill.

Silence for a moment, then, "Slip it under the door."

"It's collect," Ed squeaked.

"All right," the voice grumbled. "Wait a minute."

THERE WAS a shuffling, and the door opened a crack. Ed had his gun out, and poked it into a soft stomach. He shoved the door open and walked in, slamming it behind him.

The man in the room was immense. Tissues of fat framed the

little black eyes that squinted at Ed. He backed away from Ed's gun. "Who are you?" he stuttered.

"My name is Race," Ed grinned. "This happens to be my room. Sorry if I disturbed you."

"*Your* room? There must be a mistake. I—I thought it was my—"

"Is that why you opened my trunk? I see you picked the lock."

"Perhaps I can explain—"

"Go ahead." Ed's grim, knife-edged voice prodded.

"I'm well-known in the city. I'm sure I can satisfy you. If you'll call the desk and have them send up a policeman—"

"So you can squirm out of a jam, huh? Nix, Snead. I'm not falling for any of that."

Snead paled. "You—you know me?"

"Sure. And I know you're up here to work some kind of a frame on me. What I can't figure out is why you should come yourself." He bent to the trunk. "Let's see what you've been up to."

In the top drawer of the open trunk was the box that contained the six heavy revolvers that were part of his juggling act. Five of the revolvers were in their place, wrapped in chamois. The sixth was on the floor beside the trunk.

Ed picked up the forty-five and examined it. His eyes narrowed. He sniffed at it, then broke it and examined the chamber. "One shot fired," he said. "And recently. There's still the odor of powder." He pocketed his other gun. Now, almost unconsciously, from force of habit, he began to toss the heavy revolver in the air, catching it by the butt. He was thinking hard.

19

"I wouldn't be surprised," he said, "if this is the gun that killed Judge Hepley. I can see the idea now. One of your detectives was up here this morning and got this out of the trunk. The killer used it on Judge Hepley, then brought it back to you. He was hurt, where I shot him, so you had to come yourself to plant it in my trunk again. And here it would be when my room was searched; it would coincide with the bullet from the judge's body, and I would be in a perfect spot for the fall guy. That's why Barney tried to get me out of the way this morning—so I wouldn't even have an alibi!"

As he spoke, he kept tossing the revolver in the air. Almost mechanically, he reached out his hand to catch it; and at that moment Snead launched his two hundred and thirty pounds at him, with a low cry of rage. The force of his attack threw the fat man heavily onto the open trunk. Snead's hand darted to a pocket and came out with a gun. Snead leveled the weapon. Ed gave him no time, dived at his feet. His shoulder caught the fat politician in the stomach, and sent him hurtling back into the trunk. Ed was right after him, and wrested the gun from his hand.

The fight was knocked out of Snead. He lay there, panting for breath. Ed yanked a sheet off the bed, twisted it into a rope, and wound it three times around Snead's waist, imprisoning his arms. Then he tied a knot.

"Now," he said, "we can talk about this like gentlemen!"

"Look here, Race," Snead gasped. "You're a sensible man. What's it worth to you to get out of town and forget about this whole business? How would ten grand appeal to you?"

Ed shook his head. "The only thing that will appeal to me is to get the murderer of the judge, and to find out who killed Wilson, the gambler, so I can spring Frankie Davis. I'm sure now, that the kid was framed the same as you were going to do to me. Come across with the guy's name, and we'll call it quits."

Snead said sulkily, "All right. Lieutenant Barney did it."

Ed grinned down at him, wagged his head. "Not so good, Commish'. Barney might have killed Wilson, but he couldn't have got to the judge's house before me. Somebody else did that. And I'll know him when I see him, because he's got a bullet hole in his shoulder."

"You fool!" Snead snarled. "Don't you know when you're well off? I'm offering you ten grand to drop the whole thing! What's it to you who killed who? You're only a stranger in this town!"

THERE WAS a peculiar light in Ed's; eyes. "Judge Hepley was my friend," he said. "He once did me a great favor."

Snead barked, "What of it? You'll be doing yourself a greater favor by getting out of town. You can't beat this game. You can't hold me here forever. And even without the gun, we'll convict you of Hepley's murder. The D.A. will make out a tight ease, all right. They're sweating that kid, Frankie Davis, down at headquarters now. They'll make him write out a statement that he knew the judge was afraid of you, that you had called up the judge on the long distance and threatened him. Anything'll go in this town—I own it!"

"I don't get this, at all," said Ed. "You were ready enough to cross Lieutenant Barney, and name him as Wilson's murderer— why don't you tell me the name of Judge Hepley's killer?"

Snead veiled his eyes. "I'll make that twenty thousand, Race, if you'll listen to reason."

Ed turned away. "No soap. I see where I better be doin' things. Thanks about that tip that they're working on Frankie. I'll have to look into that." He opened the door. "Well, so long. I'll be seeing you."

Snead's voice, raised in filthy threats, came through the door after he had closed it behind him. He grunted impatiently, re-entered the room, and stuffed a balled handkerchief into the fat man's mouth. Then he rolled up a thin face-towel and tied the handkerchief in place.

"You shouldn't talk so much," he reproved gently. Snead glared up at him helplessly as he left.

Downstairs, Ed winked to the desk clerk, crossed the lobby to the switchboard, and handed the girl a bill. "Listen, sweetheart," he said, "get me Inspector Mason at the Police School. If he's in the middle of a lecture, make them call him to the 'phone—I don't care how you do it."

The girl took a look at the bill, and smiled. "Depend on me, Mr. Santa Claus!"

It took about three minutes for Mason to get on the wire. Ed spoke low and earnestly, keeping an eye on the lobby meanwhile. "Look, Inspector," he demanded, "who would be in charge of the police department in case Commissioner Snead had—er—say, an accident?"

"Why," Mason told him, "Deputy Commissioner Porter would, ordinarily. But he's in the hospital for an operation, so I guess I'd be next in line, being chief inspector."

"All right," Ed said swiftly. "Snead has had that accident—or whatever you want to call it. Anyway, he's out of the picture. So you're *it!* Now, listen carefully! Get yourself about a dozen men you can trust—you told me there were some in the department. I have them meet you at headquarters *right anyway!* I'll be there, and things'll be happening. Just pile in with the boys when you see the fireworks!"

Ed hung up on Mason's excited questions, and hustled out of the hotel. He quickly covered the short distance to headquarters, where he pulled his hat down low, and went in. They would hardly be looking for him here so soon after his escape at Emmons Street, but he was wary. No one molested him as he traversed the cool ground-floor. He passed several uniformed men, and a couple of detectives, but they paid no attention to him. He walked by a door marked "Squad Room," and another marked "Fingerprint Room." He was unfamiliar with the layout of the building, and moreover, Snead had neglected to tell him just where they had Frankie Davis.

He approached the information desk, and asked the uniformed man, "Say, where have they got this Frankie Davis kid? Inspector Mason sent me up."

The uniformed man didn't even look up from his work. He said negligently, "Upstairs in the commissioner's office. Lowry and Nevins took him up there a while ago."

Ed said, "Thanks," and went upstairs. At the end of the upper corridor he found a door marked "Commissioner's Office." He pushed in, found himself in a small anteroom. The sole occupant, a uniformed cop, was dozing. He opened his eyes with a start, frowned.

Opposite the entrance was another door, marked "Private." From behind it came a buzz of excited voices.

"Whaddyuh want?" the cop demanded.

Ed said, "It's okay, bo." He opened the door and went through.

The cop shouted, "Hey! You can't go in there!"

Ed slammed the door in his face, leaned against it.

THE COMMISSIONER'S office was large, richly furnished. At the window sat a bulky man with narrow, close-set eyes. His right arm was in a sling. He turned a startled face to the door.

But Ed paid him no attention for the moment. In the center of the room a slender lad sat beside a glass-topped mahogany desk. He was disheveled, haggard-looking. Two men in plain clothes stood over him. One was big, beefy, heavy-jowled. The other was thick-set and stocky, with a square chin and a crooked noise.

Ed's gun snapped out, covering the room. The man at the window with the arm in a sling, started to get up. He thought better of it at sight of the gun, sat down again. His face was white suddenly.

The beefy detective at the mahogany desk had the young lad's hair in a cruel grip. The boy's cheek was streaked with red splotches where he had been struck repeatedly. He was moaning, saying at the same time, "Please, Mr. Lowry, I can't stand it any more. I don't know Mr. Race. I never heard Mr. Race talk to the judge!"

Nevins, the other detective, whirled at the sound of the slamming door. Lowry let his fingers slip from the boy's hair, and turned slowly. The boy slumped back in the chair, holding his hand to his cheek.

Ed Race faced the four of them with a straight-lipped smile. His eyes were cold. "Now we'll have introductions. I'm the guy you were just asking this poor kid about. The name is Race. Maybe you'd like to ask me some of those questions?"

Nevins shuffled awkwardly. "Aw, we wouldn't of hurt the kid. We were offering to get him a break on his sentence, maybe life instead of hangin', if he'd open up on the Hepley murder. Now, don't get all het up—" His eye was on Ed's gun, "We were only doing our duty."

"Yeah," said Ed. "Your duty. Now maybe you'll tell me what's what about that bird by the window with his arm in a sling?"

Lowry glowered at him. "What's it to you? You're crazy, comin' in here when the whole force is on the hunt for you! Do you expect to get out of here again, maybe?"

Ed spoke coldly, thinly. "I asked you a question. Who is that guy with the busted wing?"

Frankie Davis suddenly sat up straight "That's Marvin Snead," he piped. "The commissioner's son!"

Ed's eyes lighted in understanding. They flicked over to the man by the window. Now he saw the resemblance—paunchy stomach, thin, cruel mouth, narrow slits of eyes imbedded in a fatty, puffed-up face. But there was a certain weakness evident in Marvin's face that was not present in his father's.

Ed exclaimed, "Now I see why the commissioner wouldn't talk! His own son!"

He strode across the room, towered over Marvin Snead, put a heavy hand on his shoulder. "You're the guy I shot this morning! You're the guy that killed Judge Hepley! You killed Wilson, the gambler, too!"

Snead's face became a pasty white. "I never killed Wilson!" he shrieked.

Ed grinned down at him, lied, "Lieutenant Barney says different. Out on Emmons Street we had a little talk, and he mentioned your name."

"He's a damn liar!"

Nevins said hastily, "Don't fall for that, Marvin. Barney never talked!"

But Snead was in a sweat of panic. He rushed ahead, heedless of Nevins. "Barney killed Wilson himself! With his own gun! He still has it He couldn't get rid of it on account the number is registered and he'd have to account for it!"

"Now we're getting some place," said Ed.

There was an oath from Lowry. "The damn cub! He's spilling his head!" He leaped at Ed, reaching for a gun.

Ed swung his revolver around, and the barrel caught Nevins squarely on the chin. He let out a gasp, and collapsed.

Lowry swung behind Frankie Davis' chair, pulled a gun, too. With his left hand he reached around and seized the lad by the throat, keeping him in the chair as a shield. Then he fired.

ED HAD been standing in front of Snead. He sidestepped just before the explosion of Lowry's gun, dropped to the floor. The slug *zinged* past him, and buried itself in Snead's body. Snead screamed, let out a choked cough, moaned, and was silent.

Lowry fired twice more, quickly, but Ed had rolled away. Frankie Davis lowered his head and bit into Lowry's wrist. At the same time Ed snapped a shot under the chair at Lowry's legs. Lowry cried out in pain, but Ed couldn't tell if it was his slug or Frankie's teeth.

Suddenly from outside there came a sound of shouts, and rushing feet. The door slammed open. Inspector Mason flung into the room, followed by a dozen men.

Lowry sprang from behind the chair, wild-eyed, and dashed for the window. Mason raised a gun, but didn't dare fire, for Ed had sprung at Lowry, caught his gun-arm, and twisted him into a helpless position with a punishing grip about his middle.

One of the men with Mason stepped up and snapped handcuffs on Lowry.

Mason exclaimed, "Good grief! Who got young Snead?"

"Lowry," Ed told him. "It was meant for me, but you can call it murder just the same. Maybe Lowry'll open up now to save his own neck. The two Sneads, Barney, Nevins, and Lowry himself were all in on the deal. Barney killed Wilson. I had it from Snead's own lips. Young Snead killed Judge Hepley. If necessary, we could prove the whole thing without Lowry, but if he'll talk, it might make it a little smoother."

Mason said, "What about it, Lowry?"

Lowry nodded gloomily. "I'll talk."

Mason seemed ten years younger. He said to Ed Race, "Newbold City is certainly in your debt for this clean-up!"

Frankie Davis came over and timidly plucked Ed's sleeve. "Can I go home now, please, Mr. Race?"

Ed grinned. "Don't ask me, kid, I'm only an actor." He pointed to Mason. "Ask the new commissioner. And if they don't make him commissioner, I'll come back and clean up this town for real, what I mean!"

CUE FOR A CORPSE

E D RACE seemed to be one of those men who attract adventure. For example, there was the business of his finding the body of the naked Samoan.

The Samoan had been a young man, not more than nineteen or twenty. He had been dead about a day, and he was beginning to smell a little. There was nothing about him to indicate his nationality, and Ed didn't know when he first saw him that he was a Samoan. However, he could tell from the dusky color of the skin, from the wide nose, thick lips, and high cheekbones, that he was a native of the South Pacific.

The discovery took place in Ed's dressing room at the Ogden Theatre in Ogdensville. Ed was booked there for a full week; his act was headlined under the name of "The Masked Marksman."

The routine of the act consisted of juggling tricks with six heavy forty-five-caliber revolvers. The high spot of the performance came when Ed, juggling three of them at a time, would fire each in turn, shooting out the flames of a row of candles thirty feet across the stage.

"The Masked Marksman" had no competition in the vaudeville circuits of the country. Few of the public knew the identity of the performer who accomplished the almost impossible feats of targetry on the stage; even fewer knew that he pursued a sideline as a hobby—the hobby being that of private detection, with

his office in his hat. He held licenses as a private investigator in a half-dozen states, but he preferred to remain an amateur in crime and a professional on the stage.

However, amateur or professional, Ed's experience had never before included the finding of the naked body of a dead man in a trunk in his dressing room.

He was alone, and the first thing he did was to lock the door.

He didn't want any of the hangers-on to walk in on him and get hysterical. Then he proceeded to examine the trunk, and he made an important discovery. The trunk, the same make and style as his, was not his own. The lock had opened to his key.

The body was curled up inside it, the man's head being between his legs. Ed didn't touch the body. He closed the lid, shutting out a little of the odor, and examined the outside. The label pasted on the top was his own, but the tag tied to one of the handles read:

Consigned via Western Valley Railroad
To: Doctor Elias Licto,
No. 12 Church Street,
Ogdensville, California.

There was no sender's name or address.

What had happened was self-evident—the baggage-man somewhere along the line had made a mistake and switched tags, and Ed had got the trunk meant for Doctor Licto. Therefore, Doctor Licto must have got Ed's trunk.

Ed allowed his muscular, lanky form to relax in the chair before the dressing table. He lighted a cigarette while he thought the situation over. Manifestly, it might be considered a tactless procedure by this Doctor Licto, if Ed visited him and told him that he had the good doctor's trunk and knew its contents. The thing to do was to notify the police. They would, no doubt, be quite interested. The quick inspection that Ed had made had showed him that the death of the naked man was due to a cracked skull.

31

Ed allowed the smoke of his cigarette to trickle slowly out of his nostrils. His eyes got that faraway expression they always assumed when crime came to perch on his doorstep.

Through his door came the muted tones of a xylophone being played on the stage. That would be the Peterman Brothers, the act which immediately preceded his. They had just started, which gave him a good fifteen minutes to dope things out.

However, it seemed that he was not to be permitted even that length of time, for almost immediately there came a timid, almost furtive knock at the door.

Ed threw a glance at the trunk to make sure there was nothing about it to betray its extraordinary contents, arose, and unlocked the door. The man who came in was only about half Ed's size, very emaciated, with eyes sunk deep in his head, with his head held cocked to one side like a bird's. The man seemed very nervous, and his hands kept moving around swiftly as if there were no place for them to rest. His eyes flew to the trunk as Ed closed the door, and skipped back to his host.

He smiled ingratiatingly, showing white, even, sharp-pointed teeth. "The *señor* have not yet discovair then there's one meestake about those trunk, no?"

Ed tried to look dumb. "Mistake? What do you mean? Who are you?"

THE VISITOR executed a neat little pirouette ending in a deep bow from the waist. "Permit me, *señor*. I am the Doctor Elias Licto, to whom thees tronk, he belong. You have not open it yet?"

"I saw the tag on it," Ed said noncommittally. "If that's yours, then you must have mine."

"But yes," Licto replied eagerly. "Eef you weel allow me to remove these, my tronk, I shall be delight' to send back your own."

"Go ahead, take it." Ed was watching him closely.

The other started to thank him profusely. "My expressmen—"

"Just a minute!" Ed stopped him. "Maybe you ought to show me some proof that you're Doctor Licto. You know how these things are. Anybody could come in and say he was Doctor Licto. Not that I doubt you—"

"But, of course, *señor!*" The little man nodded his bird-like head repeatedly. "Those proof you shall have!"

His quick-moving hands fluttered around among his clothes, executed a couple of lightning-like passes, and came to rest suddenly, each holding a small automatic trained on Ed's stomach. "These, my fran', ees all the proof I have. Regretfully, I mus' use force. Turn yourself aroun', please!"

Ed Race carefully took the cigarette out of his mouth, turned around slowly. Those two guns were too steady. He was facing the door now, could hear the swift intake of the little man's breath as he came closer. Ed knew what was going to happen— he was going to get one swell wallop on the back of his head, and while he was in the land of sweet dreams, the little man would have the trunk moved out of the room.

From outside, the sound of the xylophones grew louder, burst into a swelling crescendo. The end of the Peterman Brothers' first number. Two more, then an encore; ten minutes more.

Ed felt the little man's breath hot on his neck. He would be raising his gun now, butt first, ready for the blow.

And then Ed executed one of those brilliant, swift-moving coups that he was famous for on the stage. He dropped to one knee, resting his weight on his outstretched fingertips, while he lashed out backwards with his other foot. His heel struck bone, brought a cry of pain. Ed rolled away just as the little man tumbled to the floor, pain in his eyes.

The visitor was spry, though. He swung his guns around from his awkward position on the floor. But it was no good. Ed's hand already contained a heavy forty-five, one of the six that he used on the stage, the one that he generally carried on his person. It had come out of the shoulder-holster with such blinding suddenness that the little man didn't know what it was even when the barrel caught him in the temple. Afterward he surely didn't know, for he keeled right over and lay very still.

Ed got up, dusted off his trousers. Lucky, he thought, that he could go on for his number in his street clothes; otherwise he'd be stuck, with nothing in the trunk but a corpse.

He put a practiced hand to the little man's heart and felt the beat. He was alive, but a trifle the worse for wear. Then Ed picked up the two guns, pocketed them, and went through the pockets.

He found a passport in the name of Santander Cordiba, and the picture on the passport was the likeness of the little man. There was little else except for a letter. It was addressed to "Señor D. Santander Cordiba, Island of Tutuila, Samoa, Province of New Zealand." It was from a firm of diamond dealers in New York City, and it offered Señor Cordiba the sum of seventy-five thousand dollars in cash on delivery of the "Pearl of Samoa, if, as, and when recovered."

Ed stuffed the passport and the letter into his own pocket, dragged the unconscious form of Señor Cordiba over to the bed, and handcuffed him to the post. He got the handcuffs out of the little black overnight bag which stood on his dressing table. He seldom went anywhere without that bag. It contained, besides the handcuffs, a number of gadgets of Ed's own devising which he had found very useful since he began to delve into crime.

Through his door he heard a ripple of applause in the house— the end of the Peterman act. And almost at the same time the assistant manager knocked at his door: "Two minutes, Mr. Race!" ED CALLED out, "Okay," and went to the door, snatching up from the dressing table the little black mask he wore during the act. He had no particular reason for concealing his identity in this way, but the booking agent who handled him had originally suggested the mask as a means of titillating the public fancy, and it had been so successful that he had continued to use it.

He cast a last glance over the room, grinned at the heavy-breathing, still unconscious Señor Cordiba, and went out.

Just off the stage, most of the artists were gathered, watching the xylophonists. Norma Maitland, whose full-bodied contralto voice Ed always took pleasure in hearing, was there, and a half dozen others. As Ed had guessed, the doorman was also there. Señor Cordiba would have had little if any difficulty in removing the trunk from the theatre.

The Petermans were giving a second encore, tapping their way skillfully through the closing bars of *The Daring Young Man on the Flying Trapeze* to the accompaniment of Jerry Peterman's melodious tenor. They finished, took their last bow, and backed into the wings.

The little cardboard signs in the frames at either side of the stage slid down to reveal the name "The Masked Marksman." The spotlight for the Petermans clicked off, and the big dome under the roof blazed up, lighting the entire house. Ed always gave his performance with the lights on over the house.

Norma Maitland nudged his elbow as he adjusted the mask over his face. "Look at the man in the orchestra box, Ed. He—scares me."

Ed laughed, patted her arm. "Probably the local banker out for a big time."

The tempo of the music changed. Ed stepped out and bowed, straightened to a light ripple of applause. He walked to the table in the center of the stage on which the big revolvers were laid out. Beyond the table, at the other end of the stage, stood a tall wooden horse with twelve lighted candles.

Ed picked up three of the forty-fives, stepped to the foot-lights; the music ceased as he began to juggle. This was child's play to him, a feeling-out of the audience. He could think of other things while his hands and fingers worked mechanically, synchronizing perfectly with every muscle of his body. His mind now was on the corpse in the trunk, on the genial, murderous Señor Cordiba. Why, he wondered, should anybody ship a dead body in a trunk? The answer to that could be the obvious one—to get rid of it. But why, again, should Señor Santander Cordiba go to the extent of posing as Doctor Licto, of making violent gunplay, in order to get possession of the body?

The music speeded up, and Ed mechanically went on with the routine of the act, placing his left hand behind his back and juggling the three guns with one hand. Next would come the complete somersault while they were all three in the air.

Ed remembered what Norma had said to him, and his eye strayed to the box she had indicated. The man who sat there was not particularly terrifying. He had a little goatee, a waxed moustache; he was tall, hair carefully slicked back. His head was thin, long, his mouth a slash of red between moustache and beard. Norma's instinct was usually right. And with corpses in trunks....

The orchestra leader tapped with his baton, and the music swung into a lilting rhythm. Automatically Ed sent the three guns high into the air, back-flipped, came to his feet, and caught them, one after the other. The music crashed to a close, almost drowned by the applause.

When he straightened to go on with the act, he frowned. The man in the box had arisen and was making his way out. Was there any significance in it?

Ed went on with the routine. Twelve minutes more. At the last, when he snuffed the candles unerringly with the heavy slugs from the forty-fives, he brought down the house. He bowed his way into the wings, turned and tapped Norma Maitland encouragingly on the shoulder. She was on next. "Go to it, girlie," he told her.

While the curtain was going up again, and the house was darkening, she turned a troubled face up to him. "It's funny, Ed, how I felt about that man. He went out soon after you started—"

"Forget it." Ed gave her a little shove out onto the stage, and hurried back toward his room. The doorman, still in the wings, grinned at him.

"Great stuff, Mr. Race. I wish I could shoot like that!"

"*I* wish," Ed surprised him by replying, "that you would stick by the entrance instead of hanging around here!"

Ed made his way backstage, tried the door of his room. It was unlocked. He had left it locked. He snaked his gun out, shoved the door wide open, and stopped stock still in the doorway. His eyes narrowed as he stepped in, closed the door behind him.

The trunk was gone. Señor Santander Cordiba was still there. But Señor Cordiba was quite dead....

HE LAY sprawled on the floor at the foot of the bed, and there was a pool of blood around his head. Somebody had bashed it in for him. He was still warm, as Ed knelt and touched his gory face.

Ed stood up swiftly, surveyed the room. It was a small room, and there was no place for anybody to hide in it. Whoever had taken the trunk and finished off Señor Cordiba was gone. Ed wasted no time there, but made for the door, went out into the little corridor off the stage-entrance. The police must be notified now. He regretted that he hadn't done it before. There would be complications now. He would have a hard time convincing the local Sherlocks that he wasn't responsible for Cordiba's death. They'd certainly give him the ha-ha if he tried to convince them that a trunk with a dead man in it had vanished from the room.

The 'phone was in a booth. Ed stepped into it, lifted the receiver and started to insert a nickel. But he didn't put the nickel in. Instead he slowly hung up the receiver. For something hard was boring into his back, and a low, smooth voice was saying, "May I suggest that you do not make that call, Mr. Race?"

Ed turned his head slightly, saw the tall gentleman with the goatee who had left the box in the orchestra. He was smiling slightly now, and his red lips were parted to show a pointed tongue. There were two other men behind him, and they completely filled the narrow corridor outside the 'phone booth.

"If you will be so good as to step out—backward," said the goateed gentleman.

Ed complied. "Have I the pleasure of meeting Doctor Elias Licto?" he asked.

The gentleman with the goatee nodded. "That is my name, sir. Though it may be a doubtful pleasure for you—unless you comply with a request I'll make."

Doctor Licto motioned to the two men with him. "You, Gómez, remove Mr. Race's weapon. I believe he carries it in a shoulder holster. And you, Sardo, go to the door and see if the way is clear."

Both Gómez and Sardo were little men, like the deceased Señor Cordiba. They were swarthy, with black, lusterless eyes. They might almost have been twins, except that Gómez was a bit stouter-paunched than Sardo.

Sardo nodded, backed away toward the door, peered out into the alley alongside the theatre. Gómez reached up and yanked out the big forty-five, looked at it admiringly, and put it in his coat pocket. He himself was holding a small automatic with a silencer. Doctor Licto was still behind Ed, poking a gun into his back.

"Now," said Doctor Licto, "we will go out, if you please." He emphasized his order with additional pressure of the gun in Ed's back, and Ed went out after Gómez, with the doctor bringing up the rear. The last thing he heard as he stepped into the alley was Norma Maitland's voice taking the low notes of *Home on the Range*.

It was night outside, and Ed could distinguish the form of Sardo getting into the driver's seat of an undertaker's truck that stood at the curb just opposite the mouth of the alley.

Gómez got into the rear, and Ed climbed in with Doctor Licto's gun still at his back. These men were no novices, for they took precautions. As Ed scrambled in, any idea he might have had of making a swift play for freedom was dissipated, for Gómez knelt inside the truck and clicked a flashlight full on him.

Licto followed him in. The trunk they had taken from the dressing room was inside, and Gómez sat on it, dangling his automatic in one hand while he kept the flash on Ed's face with the other.

Licto closed the rear door, called out, "All right, Sardo."

The gears meshed; the truck moved.

Ed blinked and said quietly, "This may turn out to be very embarrassing for you, Doctor Licto. I hate being snatched."

"A thousand pardons, sir," came Licto's oily voice. "You must forgive me. There is one thing I wish from you, and then I can put an end to this inconvenience for you."

"What is that?" Ed asked. He knew that Licto was not fool enough to leave alive a man who could testify about the death of Cordiba and about the body in the trunk. But he was feeling his way.

The truck came to an abrupt halt. Doctor Licto said, "We will discuss that in my house, sir. If you will please step out now—"

He opened the door, stepped down, and waited for Ed. The truck had pulled up in a rear driveway of a private house.

Ed shrugged and stepped out. Licto nudged him with the gun. "That way, please. Up those back steps."

THEY WENT up the back steps, and the door was opened from within by another swarthy man the same size as Gómez and Sardo. Doctor Licto said, "We will go directly to the laboratory, Miguel."

The swarthy man said nothing, but turned and led the way up a flight of stairs. Gómez and Sardo came after them, carrying the trunk. At the head of the stairs was an open door through which Ed saw the interior of a superbly equipped operating room. There was an operating table at one wall, and instrument cabinets lined the others.

Miguel preceded them in, and after Ed and Doctor Licto, Gómez and Sardo carried the trunk in, brought it up close to the operating table, as if they knew just what they had to do.

Licto faced Ed with the gun in his hand. He was not smiling anymore. "I will now make my request. I wish you to give me the letter which you took from the person of Señor Cordiba."

"Sorry," Ed lied. "I tore it up and threw it away."

"That, sir," the doctor purred, "is too bad for you—unless you can remember the name and address of the firm."

"I have a terrible memory, Doc. I couldn't recall it on a bet."

Licto stared at him attentively for a long time. He said softly, "No doubt your memory can be spurred, Mr. Race. I have various means, not all of them pleasant. I am sure a sensible man like you would prefer to mention such a little thing as a name and address rather than have things done to him—things that are really painful, you know."

Ed shrugged. "Looks like I'm not sensible, Doc."

"All right!" Licto snapped. "We will continue this conversation later. Now you must excuse me." He glanced toward the trunk. "I have some work to do." He ordered the two men who had brought the trunk in, "Gómez! Sardo! Conduct Mr. Race to my office and remain there with him till I am through. You, Miguel, will help me here."

Gómez and Sardo each took a grip on one of Ed's arms, led him out of the room. Each held a silenced automatic against his ribs.

Licto called after them, "Be careful. Do not let him escape. I will hold you both personally responsible."

The office was down the hall, at the front of the house. Gómez and Sardo sidled in after Ed, took positions on either side of the door. The room was small; it contained a glass-topped mahogany desk, a swivel-chair behind the desk, and another chair alongside it. The walls were lined with bookcases.

Ed walked over to the window and looked out. The street was

dark, but he could discern that they were in a residential section; the street was a quiet one with widely-spaced private houses, large trees in front of them.

Gómez stirred uneasily, moved his gun a little forward. "Come back from the window!" he ordered. "Or I shoot!"

Ed grinned, walked back to the desk and sat on the glass top facing his two captors. "What's the boss doing in there with the corpse?" he asked. "What's he want that trunk for?"

Gómez cast a startled side glance at Sardo, then eyed Ed. "You know w'at es een the tronk?"

"Sure. Why's the boss want the corpse?"

Gómez looked again at Sardo, who nodded his head lugubriously. "You know, then. That is too bad."

Ed sighed. "I get the idea. I know—so I die. No?"

"Yes," they chimed in chorus.

"Well, well. I guess I'll have to write my will." He started to put his hand in his pocket, but Gómez took a step nearer, his fist tightening on the automatic. "No, no! No tricks. Keep the hands out!"

"Okay, okay. Just wanted a cigarette."

"Nevair mind. Just sit still."

Ed's hand played around on the desktop behind him, felt an inkwell. Gómez and Sardo couldn't see what he was doing because his body screened the inkwell. He gripped it a moment in his long, powerful fingers, and flipped it from the glass top of the desk. It rose in a swift arc, straight for Gómez' head, spattering ink in a far-flung spray. For an instant, Gómez and Sardo were surprised, and in that second Ed went backward, feet in the air, and did a back-flip over the desk. He smashed into the swivel-chair behind the desk, pulled it over with him to the floor just as the automatics of both the two captors *spatted* furiously. Slugs crashed into the wall over his head, accompanied by oaths from the two men.

Ed crept under the desk, saw a pair of legs, and yanked at them. They were Sardo's. Sardo cried out and toppled over. Ed tangled with him, rolled over and over on the floor. Gómez was dancing over them looking for an opening. Ed twisted savagely on Sardo's wrist, and the little man dropped his gun. Ed snatched it, sprang up and away just in time to avoid a wicked blow that Gómez had aimed at his head.

GÓMEZ TRIED to swing after him, but Ed gripped the sleeve of his coat, pulled hard, brought Gómez' head within reach, and brought down the automatic hard. Gómez sighed, and gave up, sprawled on the floor, dropping his gun. Sardo clawed for it, but Ed swung once more, and Sardo became quite useless.

Ed got to his feet and brushed off his trousers. He wondered how many more times tonight he would have to brush off his trousers.

The two little men lay very quiet.

Ed went to the desk, opened the drawers, inspected the papers he found there. One of these papers interested him greatly. It was a cablegram dated a week previous from the island of Samoa. It read as follows:

DOCTOR ELIAS LICTO
OGDENSVILLE, CALIFORNIA
SAMOAN DIVER SAILING TODAY CORDIBA TOO
STOP CANNOT FIND IT STOP CORDIBA IS AFTER
IT ALSO BUT HE HAS NOT GOT IT YET STOP I
WILL FOLLOW BOTH.

MIGUEL

Then there was another paper, a yellow Marconigram from the S.S. *Queen of the Pacific*, en route from New Zealand to San Francisco. It was also from Miguel.

KNOW WHERE PEARL IS BUT CANNOT GET IT
MYSELF STOP CORDIBA ON BOARD ALSO KNOWS
STOP AM SHIPPING YOU TRUNK BE CAREFUL OF
CONTENTS.

The Marconigram was dated the day before yesterday. Ed knew that the *Queen of the Pacific* had arrived at Frisco the day before, for he had come to Ogdensville on the train with a couple of people from her. That explained the trunk incident. The ship had docked, the trunk had been piled on with Ed's, and the mistake had been made by the baggage-man.

But why should Miguel have shipped Doctor Licto the body of the Samoan? Evidently he had killed him in his search for the pearl. But why not dump it over the side?

Suddenly, Ed snapped his fingers as a great light broke. He stuffed the two cables in his pocket, stepped over the bodies of Gómez and Sardo, and stole down the corridor toward the laboratory. The fight in the office had not caused interference from down the corridor. Evidently Doctor Licto and Miguel were very busy and were confident that two armed men were more than a match for Race.

Ed tried the door, found it open, and stepped in, one of the silenced guns in his hand.

Licto was dressed in an operating robe, and Miguel wore a smock. The doctor held a bloody scalpel, with which he had been carving the body of the dead Samoan. They had put him up on the operating table, and he looked gruesome enough, curled up into the position he had been in while in the trunk, his abdomen sliced open. The place looked like an abattoir.

Doctor Licto grunted, "Have to kill him?" over his shoulder. Then, as Ed kept silent, he turned, gasped in astonishment. He dropped the scalpel, but clutched tightly at something he had in his other hand.

Miguel frowned too, snarled, took a crouching step toward Ed, but stopped when he saw the muzzle of the gun staring at him. Licto said, "It appears that you are a very surprising young man."

"Thanks for the compliment," Ed grinned. "Now, hold everything."

HE STEPPED to the telephone in the corner, lifted the receiver, and asked for police headquarters. When he got the connection, he asked to have the homicide squad sent over.

"Homicide squad!" the desk man at headquarters snorted. "What do you think this is—Frisco? We ain't got a homicide squad! What is it, a murder?"

"Something like that. If you have no homicide squad, send

over a bunch of cops—and a wagon—the morgue wagon—*and* the coroner!"

Ed hung up, grinned at Licto. "How's the dissecting, Doc? You going in for vivisection?"

Licto was wiping blood from his gown. "I regret now that I didn't have you killed at once. I underestimated you."

Miguel was getting out of his smock, seeming to have difficulty getting it over his head. He finally got out of it, shed it, and his hand came clear holding a gun. Ed's eye caught the gun, and he fired a fraction of a second before Miguel.

Miguel seemed to be greatly astonished. His mouth fell open, his eyes widened, and he staggered backward. Blood from the hole in his chest pumped out in little spurts of red. His fingers relaxed, the gun fell to the floor, and Miguel followed it there; twitched, groaned, and was silent.

Doctor Licto looked on unmoved, still holding his left hand clenched over some object.

In a few minutes there was the sound of a siren outside, the screeching of brakes, loud voices, heavy feet on the stairs. A half-dozen uniformed men burst into the room, led by a stout individual in plainclothes.

The stout man puffed a moment, looked the room over, announced, "I'm Chief Broderick. What the hell's happened here?"

Ed explained tersely, while Licto stood impassive.

Broderick couldn't get it. "But what's the idea?" he protested. "Why did this Miguel ship the dead body? An' why did that dead guy back there in the theatre want to get hold of the trunk?"

"The way I figure it," Ed continued, his eyes on Licto, "the Samoan was a diver employed by some pearler out there. He found this pearl, tried to get away with it by swallowing it. Cordiba tried to get him away, but Licto's man, Miguel, was wise to the stunt, followed them, and searched the cabins. When he couldn't find the pearl, he figured that the Samoan had swallowed it, so he just killed the Samoan and shipped his body to Licto."

Ed stepped over, gripped Licto's wrist, twisted, and the doctor's hand opened under the pressure. A blood-stained, round object fell to the floor.

"There's the pearl, Chief!" Ed said.

THE DEATH JUGGLER

THE MESSAGE to stop in at Ma Gibson's had been urgent. Ed Race had picked it up at the desk at the Longmont Hotel, where he always stayed when he played New York.

Earlier in the day, immediately after checking in at the Longmont, he had brought the big forty-fives that he used in his star vaudeville juggling act over to Ma Gibson's place, to be thoroughly overhauled. She ran a little old-fashioned gunsmith and repairing shop on Forty-fifth Street, and Ed never failed to have her go over his revolvers when he hit town.

Now he wondered why she had left so urgent a message. He couldn't call her up, for she had no 'phone in the place, so the only thing to do was to go there.

However, he did not head directly for his destination; there was something else that had been on his mind all day and which he decided to take care of now.

For he knew that he had been trailed ever since he arrived at Grand Central Station; trailed by a man who stuck like a leech, but had not been particularly successful in concealing the fact.

Ed stopped now under the marquee of the Grand Theater, sensed rather than saw that his shadow had stopped not ten feet behind him. Ed glanced up at the electric sign over the entrance, which flashed his own name—*The Masked Marksman*. Ed still got a thrill out of seeing himself up in the bright lights in the Big Town. His specialty act was deservedly headlined. It consisted of juggling the six heavy forty-fives to which he gave such loving care—juggling them as guns had never been juggled before, with the climax of the act coming when he had three of the revolvers in play in the air at once, and shot out the flames of a row of candles thirty feet across the stage with each gun in turn as it came down into his hand. The Masked Marksman was in a class by himself in vaudeville.

Not even the fact that he had a sideline which furnished plenty of excitement could wean him away from his first love— the stage. His sideline was that of private detective, and though Ed Race held licenses to operate in a dozen states, he preferred to revel in the crashing plaudits of a packed house night after night, as he performed his miraculous feats of dexterous juggling and unequalled marksmanship behind the warm footlights.

Now as he stood under the marquee of the Grand, his mind was divided between the electric sign and the problem of why he was being shadowed. Ed was in New York now, though it was not in his regular schedule until January, through a special rearrangement of his bookings at the request of the District Attorney's office; he was wanted to testify as a witness in a case on the calendar of the Court of General Sessions for that week. Perhaps this trailer....

Ed noted his shadow out of the corner of one eye, glanced at his wristwatch. It was eight-thirty—almost two hours before he had to go on. His eyes gleamed as he stepped up to the ticket booth, counted out eighty-three cents, and got a ticket. His trailer would no doubt think he was crazy—paying admission

to the show he was appearing in. In the glass of the booth he saw the man's reflection; he had joined the line right behind him. Ed nudged with his arm at the forty-five strapped under his left armpit, and stepped back heavily, the heel of his shoe crushing into the man's instep.

His maneuver was rewarded with a bellow of rage. The man, his face contorted with pain, reached out and gripped Ed by the shoulder. "Get off my foot, you monkey!" he howled.

Ed got off the foot, whirled around, and gripped the man by

the front of his coat. He said very calmly, "You shoved me and you called me names. I'm not a monkey." The man was heavy, but Ed shook him easily, his fingers retaining their grip on his coat lapels. "I'm going to call a policeman and have you arrested for using abusive language."

THE EVENING throngs were pouring into Broadway at this hour, and it took no time for a crowd to gather. Ed saw Detective Sergeant Bland shoving through the crowd, and started to grin.

Bland demanded, "What's this, anyway?" Then he saw Ed Race and the other man, and his face fell; he looked sheepish.

Ed, still clutching the man's coat, said, "Hello, Steve. This man shoved me and used abusive language. It's terrible the way some people have no manners."

Bland glared at the man Ed was holding, took Ed's arm and guided them both into the lobby of the theater. When they were away from the crowd Bland said to the heavy man, "You're a hell of a trailer, Grogan. Here I drag you all the way in from Richmond so we'll have someone that Race wouldn't remember, and the first crack out of the box, he spots you!"

Grogan stared murderously at Ed, mumbled, "He stepped on my foot. I'll break his neck."

Ed said nothing, grinning broadly as if he was enjoying himself. Bland shrugged disgustedly. "All right, Grogan. Beat it back to the precinct house and report out. You can go home. You're no damn good here anymore." He gave the plainclothes man a little shove, and sent him on his way.

Ed kept on grinning, extracted a cigarette from a pack, offered one to Bland, who waved it away impatiently. "Look, Race," he burst out, "I only put the tail on you for your own good. Tomorrow, Orpen goes on trial for murder and kidnapping. It took us almost a year to catch him, and you're the people's star witness."

Bland poked a finger up, wagged it in Ed's face, and went on. "But you know damn well that Orpen's got powerful backing—you know as well as I, that he isn't the Big Gun. It's Pete Lucie that really figured out that snatch racket for Orpen; only nobody can touch Lucie. And Lucie isn't going to let his man take the rap—if only to keep up his reputation." Bland stopped a minute, regarded Ed with smoldering eyes. "You're a crazy fool for walking the streets tonight, for even thinking about stepping onto the stage of this theater tonight. You won't live till morning if you don't have some kind of protection."

Ed flicked the ash from his cigarette. "So you give me that ham of a Grogan? Thanks. I can do better by myself. When I yell for help it'll be plenty time for you to butt in."

Bland bit his lip. "I've half a mind to take you in and hold you till tomorrow. You'll be a hell of a lot safer in a cell tonight."

"Why don't you try it, Steve?" Ed asked softly. "I can tell you right now that my act goes on tonight—Lucie or no Lucie. I haven't missed an appearance in six years, and I'm not starting now. And if you should have any cockeyed ideas about taking me in, Steve, I warn you that the shock of being arrested would completely ruin my memory. I bet Orpen would get an acquittal without my testimony."

Bland turned away resignedly. "Don't I know it? Well, all I

can say is, take care of yourself. And after the trial—I hope you croak!"

Ed thoughtfully watched the detective sergeant's back mingle with the sidewalk throng. He was watchful now, awake to his danger; and without appearing to do so, he was inspecting the men entering the lobby of the theater. Abruptly his eyes narrowed.

Two men who had bought tickets while he was talking to Bland were crossing the lobby toward the doorman, studiously avoiding looking at him. Ed remembered them both very well— Gene Glutz and Joe Spinelli. They were two of Pete Lucie's shock troops over at the Wineland Casino on Forty-fourth, where everything went, and where Lucie made his headquarters as head of the fastest growing heroin and cocaine business in the country. Ed thought it strange that these two should suddenly exhibit an interest in vaudeville just as the Wineland was opening for the evening.

He followed them past the ticket taker, through the door, into the inside lobby. They were going slowly, side by side, toward the orchestra entrance. Ed turned right, started up the stairs toward the mezzanine. His back was to them now; he couldn't see what they were doing.

A couple was going up just ahead of Ed, the young man's hand caressingly on the girl's shoulder. A middle-aged woman appeared at the head of the stairs, on the way down. She came down toward Ed, tactfully refraining from looking at the ascending couple in front of him; instead she glanced down toward the foot of the stairs. Ed watched her, saw her eyes widen with amazement and sudden fright.

Ed stopped and whirled. His gun was out of its shoulder holster and barking with flaming streaks of death down at the figures of Glutz and Spinelli, who stood at the foot of the stairs, each with a heavy automatic in his hand!

ED'S ACTION had been a symphony of coördinated rhythm, like his timed movements on the stage. Glutz was the first one hit, and his body hurtled backward, struck the deep carpeting, bounced once, rolled, jerked, and lay still. Spinelli's gun exploded again and again as his convulsively twitching fingers contracted on it; but the muzzle was in the air, and the slugs shattered glass in the immense chandelier in the ceiling. Ed's second shot had got him just over the heart, as he was raising his gun.

The rumbling of the explosions came back from the roof of the theater, increased to a tremendous crescendo by the acoustic properties of the place. Mingled with the roaring echoes were the screams of women and the excited shouts of men. Ed turned, holstered his revolver, and dashed up the steps past the dazed couple, past the limp body of the middle-aged woman who had fainted after uttering a single shriek.

Upstairs, a wasp-waisted usher came running toward him, bewilderedly looking for the source of the trouble. He paid no attention to Ed, and the actor slipped past him into the darkness of the mezzanine. Patrons were turning uneasily in their seats, craning necks, their attention distracted from the acrobatic troupe that occupied the stage.

Ed Race made his way quietly along the rear of the mezzanine to the other side of the house. He went out into the corridor, passed two more scurrying ushers, and descended the stairs which brought him out at the Forty-third Street exit.

A radio car was screaming its way east against the one-way traffic. Ed ducked across the street after it passed, and headed west, walking quickly, but not fast enough to attract attention. It would have been foolhardy to remain behind to be picked up by the police. The shooting was as clear a case of self-defense as could be found, but even if he had been able to bulldoze Bland into letting him go, it would have meant a trip down to headquarters, delay, while Ma Gibson was waiting for him.

He passed rapidly growing numbers of people hastening toward Broadway, attracted by the radio car sirens and by the sight of the crowd that had formed as if by magic in front of the Grand Theater. He turned the corner into Eighth Avenue, went up to Forty-fifth, and walked over a half-block. He descended three steps into a dimly lit store in the basement of a private house. The built-in window of the store was littered with junk, knickknacks and guns. The only lettering on the window was the name, *Gibson's*.

The store was long and narrow, with a small counter at the rear. When the door opened, a bell jangled upstairs. A moment later heavy footsteps sounded, the curtain behind the counter parted, and a big woman appeared.

She weighed fully two hundred and ten pounds, and she waddled. She had four chins and pinpoint eyes, but there was a smile of good nature on her face that made one forget the fat.

She was comparatively young, perhaps not over forty, and her black hair was combed severely back from her ears, which looked ridiculously small in juxtaposition to the rest of her.

Ed said, "Hello, Ma, anything wrong? Are my guns ready?"

She nodded. Though her eyes reflected nothing of what she felt, there was deep perturbation in her voice. "They're ready, Ed. But it wasn't about that. I shouldn't really have called you; but I couldn't help it—I was so worried. It's about—Judy!"

Though he had never met her, Ed had heard much about Judy, Ma Gibson's only daughter, whom she supported at boarding school out of the small income she derived from the store.

"What about her?" he asked. "I hope she's not in any trouble."

"It may be, Ed. She always writes me twice a week, and I write her. You know, I never have her come home for the holidays; I'm always afraid that somebody'll whisper in her ear that her mother was once—"

"Never mind," Ed said hastily. "Let's not mention it. You've quit all that now."

"Thanks to you, Ed." She leaned over the counter, and there was a depth of emotion in her face that one would not have thought possible. "Thanks to you, I've been able to bring Judy up like a lady. But now, I don't know—"

She stopped, and gulped.

"Go on," Ed urged. "Tell me all about it."

"Well, she hasn't written for a week, hasn't answered my letters. Today, I got to worrying, and I went out and called up the school on the long distance. And what do you think, Ed?

They told me that Judy hasn't been there all day. She hasn't been seen since last night! They were writing to me about it today!"

ED SAID, "There must be a logical explanation of it. Tell you what I'll do. Tonight, after the show, I'll take a late train up there, and look the situation over—provided she hasn't been heard from by then."

Ma Gibson said fervently, "Thanks, Ed. I knew you'd do it. I—can't go myself. I don't want her swell chums to see—what kind of a mother Judy has!"

Ed lowered his yes. "All right, Ma, that's settled. Now—" He took out his revolver—the one he had used in the Grand—and laid it on the counter. "Bury that for me."

She picked up the revolver, looked at him with troubled eyes. "You in a jam, Ed?" Suddenly she put a pudgy hand on his sleeve. "It ain't that Glutz and Spinelli killing, is it? I got it on the shortwave."

"Never mind, Ma," Ed rebuked her. "Just get to work."

He lit a cigarette and waited for her to return. Soon there came the *whirring* of an electric file from behind the curtain, and after a few minutes she came back, put the revolver down on the counter.

"That'll fool 'em," she said. "I filed the breech smooth, then I put a couple of extra furrows in it. If they get this gun down in the ballistics bureau, it'll never shoot a bullet like any that it ever shot before. You practically got a new gun, Ed, but with the same number." At the same time she lifted a neatly wrapped parcel from under the counter, handed it over to him. "There's your six regulars, all cleaned and oiled."

Ed put a fifty-dollar bill on the counter and started out. "Don't worry any about Judy, Ma Gibson," he called back to her. "I'll start up there tonight."

He worked his way back to Eighth, then down again to Forty-fourth, keeping a wary eye on the passing crowds, as well as on cars that might house machine-gunners. Pete Lucie would know about the Grand Theater business by this time; would, no doubt, be trying again. Lucie was not the kind of man to give up—especially in a matter like this.

However, nothing happened, and Ed walked unmolested into the Wineland Casino—Lucie's headquarters. He looked at his wristwatch. Nine-fifteen—plenty of time before he'd have to go on at the Grand.

The town was coming to life; taxis were depositing parties at the Casino door; the gay strains of dance music came from the dining room on the first floor.

Ed crowded into the elevator with half a dozen other people, remained there while most of them got off at the dining-room floor. Two men who seemed bent on a wild night of gambling stayed on and got off at the next floor, where the games were in progress behind steel doors. That left only Ed and one man and a woman. The woman was young, a little embarrassed; the man, eager. They got out at the fourth, where the private dining rooms were located.

The elevator operator seemed a little surprised to find he still had a passenger. Ed said, "I'll take the top."

The operator was a beefy man with coarse features, who looked out of place in the natty khaki uniform provided by the

Wineland. "There's nothing upstairs, mister," he said. "Whachu want—eat? That's downstairs."

"I want to see Pete Lucie," Ed told him. "In the office upstairs!"

The operator started the car downward. "Nobody goes up there. You'll have to talk to the manager on the second floor."

"Suppose we cut the argument short," Ed suggested. He poked his revolver into the man's ribs.

The operator stiffened when he felt the gun, brought the car to a halt between the third and fourth floors. He turned slowly, surveyed Ed. "What is this, a stickup?"

"Hell, no. Just a little social call. I'm Ed Race. I thought I'd step in and save Lucie the trouble of sending out for me."

The man stared at him, then shrugged. "Race, huh? I heard you was crazy." He pushed the lever over, shot the car upward again. "Well, you're askin' for it. It'll be your own funeral."

At the top Ed got out, waited while the operator closed the gate and shot the cage downward. The last thing he saw as the gate closed was the broken-toothed grin of mockery on the operator's face.

ED WAS in a narrow corridor. In the wall opposite were a small grilled window, and, a few feet to the left, a heavy door. There was nobody at the window. Ed peered through it and saw that it opened into a sort of anteroom. Beyond the anteroom was a short hall with another door at the end.

Just beneath the window was a small monitor switchboard. It started to buzz with an incoming call, and Ed put down on the floor his package with the oiled revolvers, reached a hand in, depressed the end key, and lifted the headset from its hook on the board.

"Hello," he said.

The voice of the elevator operator came to him. "Hello, Ryker? Say, that was Ed Race himself I just took up. I couldn't help it—he put a gun to my back. Do you want I should send some of the boys up?"

Ed growled, "No!" disguising his voice. "Leave this floor alone till you're called."

He clicked the key up, replaced the headset on its hook. Then he went to the door and tried it. It was locked. His little black bag, containing instruments that would have opened the lock without difficulty, was back at the hotel, where it could do him no good now.

He returned to the grilled window, reached in and depressed the operator's key. Then he pressed the key just beneath it, and the 'phone bell on the monitor board began to ring. Ed kept his finger on the bell key for a moment, rang it again, then pulled his arm out from between the bars of the window and pressed himself against the wall, taking his revolver out again.

In a minute the door at the far end of the hall opened, and a stocky, broad-shouldered man came out, calling back into the room, "It was ringing in here, Chief. That dopey dame must have forgot to connect the board inside."

The stocky man closed the connecting door and came over to the switchboard. He bent to lift the headset, and Ed stuck his gun through the grille-work. The muzzle just touched the man's temple, and he sprang back with a startled oath.

61

"Take it easy, Mister Ryker," Ed said.

Ryker gasped. "How the hell did you get up here, Race?"

"That's another one of those puzzles." Ed's voice became curt. "Just walk over and unlock that door from the inside. *Without* arguments!" he added as the other raised his hand in a gesture of refusal.

Ryker looked into Ed's steady eyes, lowered his gaze, and went to the door. He unlocked it, swung it open. "What now?" he asked sulkily.

Ed had his gun through the grille, trained on Ryker. "Now," he ordered, "lift those mitts of yours over your head and stand still."

Ryker raised his hands. Ed withdrew his arm from the grille, leaped to the doorway.

But Ryker had taken advantage of the moment during which he was not covered. His hand flashed down toward his armpit. Ed came through the open doorway just as Ryker's gun was halfway out. Ed didn't hit him with his revolver; but acting with the speed which had made his motions on the stage resemble masterpieces of swift precision, he drove his left fist out into Ryker's face in a pistonlike blow.

Ryker was catapulted backward into a filing cabinet. The cabinet tipped under the sudden impact and went down over on the floor with a resounding crash. Ryker joined the cabinet on the floor and lay still.

Ed stepped into the office after him, just as the connecting door at the far end of the short hall was thrown open. The man who stood in the doorway was tall, thin almost to emaciation, with deep-sunk eyes and gaunt cheeks—Pete Lucie.

He, too, had a gun in his hand. His eyes flicked from the unconscious Ryker, sprawled over the cabinet, to Ed. He said in a cold, precise voice, "What do you want, Race?"

Ed smiled thinly. "Your friends—Glutz and Spinelli—" he told Lucie, "have been trying to use me for a target. It gave me an idea for a new routine for my act… I'm going to practice making a human sieve—and I'm starting with you."

LUCIE'S FACE paled. He started to raise his gun. Ed had his revolver swinging easy in his hand, waiting for the other's gun to come up before raising it to fire. But Lucie suddenly lowered his gun.

"Let's talk about it, Race," he said in the same expressionless voice.

"Okay," Ed told him. "Make your speech."

Lucie was silent for a moment, appraising the actor-detective. He was a keen judge of human nature, which accounted for his success and power. Finally he spoke, making his bid for truce.

"It's true, Race," he said, "that I've—sent the boys after you. Glutz and Spinelli were only the first—teasers, sort of. I've already worked out another stunt for taking care of you. In fact, I've been planning it for a week now, and it's sure-fire—*even if I should get killed!* The works are in for you, Race. It's impossible for you to live till morning unless I, personally, change the plans. Will you take fifty grand in cash and leave New York *now?*"

Ed shook his head. "I've got a show on tonight, Lucie. And besides, Orpen was a dirty, double-crossing skunk, and

I'm giving my testimony in court tomorrow—and taking my chances on your plans. And maybe Orpen will open up when he faces the chair, and maybe that'll be the end of Pete Lucie."

Slowly and carefully Lucie put his gun back in his pocket, making sure that his hand didn't jerk when he did it. "I've seen your act on the stage, Race," he said then, "and I'm not trading shots with you. If you came here to kill me, it'll do you no good. You shoot me now, and there'd be a hundred people up here in a minute. My body'd be found without a gun in my hand—and you can't get away with cold-blooded murder."

Ed had no chance to answer, for the elevator door out in the corridor clanged open. He glanced through the grilled window, and hastily pocketed his revolver. For Detective Sergeant Bland and another plainclothes man had stepped out of the cage.

Lucie's face broke into a smile of relief. He exclaimed, as Bland stepped through the doorway, "You certainly are welcome, Sergeant! This madman was beginning to get on my nerves."

Bland nodded curtly to Lucie, and said glumly to Ed, "I guessed you'd come up here. It's just like a crazy actor. Sorry, Ed, but I got to place you under arrest for the killing of Glutz and Spinelli. Let's have your gun."

"Sure," Ed grinned. He handed over the revolver.

Lucie stepped forward. "Look here, Sergeant, this man knocked out Ryker here, and threatened to kill me—said he'd make a human sieve out of me. It's a good thing you came when you did!"

Bland grunted as he led Ed Race out. "I'm damn sorry I

didn't get held up five minutes or so. It would be a good thing for the town."

Lucie had recovered his poise. Disregarding Bland, he called after Ed, "Don't forget to be careful tonight, Race—in case they don't put you in jail!"

JOHN HAGAN, Inspector of Homicide, looked more like an insurance salesman than a cop. He was a man of slight build who affected an extreme nattiness of dress. His blue serge, double-breasted suit was always carefully pressed, while his tie, socks and shirt always matched in an appropriate shade of blue. His passion for blue was carried out further in the handkerchief that peeped out of his breast pocket.

Ed Race, who, being an actor, might have been expected to be careful of his appearance, made a striking contrast to the inspector in his rumpled gray suit, white shirt and nondescript tie. He sat on the desk now, grinning down at Hagan.

"I'll bet you five bucks," Ed was saying, "that my gun doesn't check with the bullets that came out of Glutz and Spinelli."

Hagan glowered up at him. "Lay off the innocent stuff, Race. Bland saw you go in. You always use forty-fives. Forty-five slugs were found in both those stiffs. The old dame couldn't pick you out of the lineup because she was all broken up. It's just your luck so far, that the only one who saw the actual shooting should be a fidgety old dame." He leaned forward in the swivel chair, and his hard features twisted themselves into a smile that was a travesty of mocking sweetness. "I suppose when Bland comes up and reports that Ballistics finds it's your gun that fired the slugs, you'll be the most surprised person on earth. You just won't be able to understand how it could have happened! Haha! What a laugh that'll be!"

Ed kept on grinning. "I tell you, Hagan, you aren't going to get any kind of report like that from Ballistics."

Hagan guffawed. "The hand is quicker than the eye—yah! All you wise birds trip up. You're licked, Race." He became confidential. "Why don't you come through with the story, Race? No jury would convict you. It's a perfect S.D.—they gunned down on you, and you shot them in self-defense. Better talk now; after the report comes in I might not want to listen to you."

He looked up as the door opened and Bland came in, looking glum. He had Ed's gun, which he handed back to him. "No soap, Inspector," he told Hagan. "The slugs in Spinelli and Glutz were never fired from this gun. Maybe it was one of those." He indicated the opened package of guns which Ed had gotten at Ma Gibson's, and which they had brought along from Lucie's office.

Ed holstered the gun, stood off the desk. "Sure," he said bitterly. "If I didn't do it one way, I did it another. You know damn well those six guns haven't been fired—they're all freshly oiled and cleaned. Why don't you admit your case is as flat as a pancake? Anyway"—he poked Bland in the chest—"you guys are a swift pain in the neck. Why don't you forget about it when somebody does you a favor and rubs out two leeches like Glutz and Spinelli!"

He turned to Hagan and said, "Well, your honor—I await your apologies!"

Hagan half-rose in his chair, spluttering. "Why, you—you—"

He was saved the necessity of finding an appropriate word

by the abrupt ringing of the telephone. He glowered at Ed, then picked up the 'phone. "Hagan talking," he growled. "Yeah, he's right here. Wait a minute." He handed the 'phone to Ed. "Another stunt of cheap hybrid actors," he remarked sourly. "Having themselves paged wherever they go!"

Ed took the instrument, and his eyes snapped to attention at the first words of Ma Gibson at the other end. "Ed!" she exclaimed. And it was the first time he had heard her on the verge of hysterics. "Oh, Ed, I know you're in trouble, but there's nobody else I can call. I just got a special delivery letter from her, Ed. Do you want I should read it to you?"

Ed's voice was suddenly parched. Though he had never met Judy, he knew she was the very life of this motherly woman.

"Read it," he said huskily. He saw the eyes of both Hagan and Bland on him, but paid them no attention. "Go on, read it!"

" 'Dear Ma,' it says, 'I am quitting school. This is no place for me after what I know. I'm going to New York, but not to live with you. Ma, I've found out what you used to be; and I know who made you do it. And I can't face you till I've killed the man who made you commit crimes. I've learned all about him. I know where to meet him. After I've killed him I'll come back to you. Dear Mother, I can't stand to think of all the sacrifices you've made to keep me in school. Goodbye, Ma. I'll see you soon.'"

Ma Gibson's voice ended in a half-gasp as she finished reading. "What does it mean, Ed? I don't understand what she's talking about. There's no man that made me commit crimes. It sounds like a dope dream. Somebody's told her all about me—

and twisted the story. What'll I do? Think of Judy somewhere in the city, bent on murdering a man!"

"Take it easy, Ma," Ed soothed her. "Tell you what you do— you come over to my hotel right away. I'll meet you there. Now don't let yourself break up—it won't help you at all. There's a nice girl."

When he hung up, his mouth was a grim line. "You holding me, Hagan?" he demanded sharply.

"I suppose not," Hagan grumbled. "Just so you do your proper stuff at the Orpen trial in the morning. And don't forget, you ham actor, that I could slam you in a cell if I wanted to. So don't go around beefing that we ride you!"

Ed was wrapping up his guns. "Sure not. You love me—like a stepbrother with the mumps. The only reason you're not sticking me in the can is because you want my testimony tomorrow." Then, as Hagan started to get red in the face, he added hastily, "But don't worry—I'll go through for you." He swung around and buttonholed Bland. "You'd know about this, Steve. How's Pete Lucie's snow racket coming along? Has he been out of town in the last few weeks?"

"We can't get a thing on him on the snow angle—or any other angle, for that matter. And the Feds can't get to first base on him either. About his being out of town, he was up in Cliffside last week, and again the day before yesterday. He was tailed, but the only report I could get was that he was hanging around with some of the co-eds up there. Why? You still after him?"

Ed was on his way out. "Uh-huh."

Bland watched him disappear into the corridor, then

shrugged and turned to Hagan. "That boy is sure hard to stop when he's rubbed the wrong way. I think Lucie picked himself a Tartar this time."

"I wish the lad luck," Hagan grumbled. "He riles me at times, but—I sorta like him in spite of himself."

Bland whistled. "If you ever told that to Ed Race he'd drop dead of the shock!"

ED RACE was extremely careful on his way back to the Longmont, looking out for Pete Lucie's next offensive. But nothing happened; evidently Lucie was planning something more complicated than hired gunmen this time.

At the hotel he left his package at the desk. When he got his key the clerk said to him, "There's a girl waiting for you in the rear lounge, Mr. Race. She wouldn't give her name."

"What kind of girl?" Ed asked.

The clerk smiled knowingly. "She's about seventeen or eighteen. I didn't think she was your style, but she kept insisting she had to see you. So I told her to wait, figuring you'd probably stop in on the way to the theater. She's not bad, Mr. Race. You got good taste."

"Why don't you go and wash your brains with soap," Ed said. "You've got a dirty mind."

He went into the rear lounge. There were only two people in it as he entered. One was a girl whom he immediately recognized from pictures Ma Gibson had fondly showed him. Her long, bobbed hair was a deep, soft brown; she wore a simple tailored suit, and held a purse in her lap. It was her eyes that interested Ed; they were black, widely dilated.

The other person was a man who sat in the far corner in an easy chair, reading a newspaper. The paper was spread so that it hid the upper part of his body.

Ed came up to the end table alongside which the girl sat, rested his hands on it and said, "Did you want to see me, Miss Gibson? My name is Race."

She had watched his approach from the door, her hands moving nervously in her lap. She looked up at him now, her little mouth pressed tight, her eyes burning into his.

"Edward Race?" she asked. He nodded.

She arose, fumbling in her handbag. "Edward Race," she said as if repeating a lesson by heart, "I've come to kill you for what you did to my mother. You're a beast!"

She pulled a small, ivory-handled revolver from the purse.

Ed acted with concentrated speed. His two hands clutched the end table, and he heaved. The table went over, catching her in the legs, driving her backwards. She lost her balance, stumbled backward on her heels.

Ed let go of the end table, allowed it to fall, and leaped around it. He seized the hand which held her gun, caught her as she fell, held her helpless.

She struggled to wrench her hand free, sobbing in frustration as she realized she was beaten. Ed's arm tightened around her slim waist. His left hand squeezed until the revolver fell to the floor.

She shrieked again and again, "Damn you, damn you, damn you! I'll kill you!"

Her voice reached a high pitch of hysteria, resounding shrilly through the whole hotel. Ed slapped her hard in the face—the best treatment for hysterics.

"You little fool! You've been listening to stories! And you've been fed dope! You're out of your head!"

Suddenly she sagged in his arms.

There was a crowd milling in the doorway behind Ed. He looked up just in time to see that the man who had been reading the newspaper had arisen from the easy chair in the corner and was on the way out through the rear door. Ed started to lower the body of Judy Gibson to the chair, when the man turned.

Ed's eyes narrowed, for the man now had a handkerchief over the lower part of his face, and a gun in his hand, which he was aiming at them.

Instead of lowering the girl into the chair, Ed swung her inert body in a continuous sweep to the floor, pushed her away from him, and rolled over. His hand clutched Judy's gun, which was lying on the thick carpet, came up with it and fired once—before the other's gun exploded!

The action had been a single, continuous blur of motion— almost instinctive with Ed, for his muscles were trained to perfect coördination by daily performances on the stage.

The man in the doorway uttered a screech like a frightened hen. He jumped in the air as if stung. Then he collapsed.

Ed dropped the revolver and got to his feet. The crowd from outside stormed in now that the shooting was over, and several officious men bent over Judy.

Ed said, "She's not hurt—just fainted."

Someone brought water, and soon Judy was sitting up with

a dazed expression, as if she were coming out of a bad dream. From the doorway came a low moan, and Ma Gibson rushed to her side, cradled the girl's head in her arm.

Ed started to walk over to the dead man in the rear doorway. He stopped, heard Inspector Hagan's booming voice.

Hagan took in the scene in a twinkling, rushed past Ed and snatched the handkerchief from the dead man's face.

"It's Lucie!" he gasped.

"Yeah," said Ed. "And this time I'm not admitting I shot him—I'm boasting of it!" He glanced at his wristwatch. "Hell! I got a curtain call at the Grand in fifteen minutes!"

DEATH'S SPOTLIGHT

E D RACE saw the whole thing, and he knew it was no accident. He had finished his number at the Grand Theatre—his last before going on the road again in the morning—and was taking a fast constitutional across Forty-Second Street when it happened.

The woman was standing in front of the Public Library near the corner of Fifth Avenue, apparently watching for some one. The tall, thin man was coming across Forty-second, going the same way as Ed, but on the opposite side of the street. When he saw the woman at the corner, he started to cross in the middle of the block.

Then it happened. The car must have been following that man. As soon as he stepped off the curb it came shooting along from behind, straight for him.

The tall man turned, saw it coming, and tried to dodge back to the sidewalk, but he didn't have a chance. The big car swerved in his direction, smashed into him sickeningly.

Ed saw his face under the street lamp for an instant before he was hit. It was strangely splotched in spots; his mouth was opened to shriek. But before he could utter a sound, his body went hurtling a dozen feet, and landed inert and broken, huddled up close to the curb.

Ed obeyed his first instinct. In a motion so swift that it para-

lyzed the eyes, he had drawn the heavy forty-five from the holster under his left armpit, and had it leveled. He was going to shoot one of the tires, cripple that car so it couldn't escape. But he didn't fire. For, instead of attempting to escape, the car had pulled up short.

Both front doors opened, and two men jumped out. They both wore baggy topcoats and soft felt hats. They hastened toward the injured man and knelt beside him, bending over very close.

Ed's blood tingled. He was a vaudeville actor by profession. He juggled revolvers on the stage, and performed feats of marksmanship with his six famous forty-fives that few men could equal. He was known from coast to coast in vaudeville circuits as "The Masked Marksman." But in private life he indulged a hobby that was far more thrilling to him—he held licenses in a dozen states as a private detective. And that hobby had provided him in the past with many a moment of blood-tingling excitement. This promised to be one of them.

Ed noted that the woman who had been waiting in front of the library was running across the street now. He holstered his revolver, headed in that direction too. A crowd was forming swiftly. Ed got there about the same time as the woman. His keen glance noted something strange; one of the two men from the car, shielded by his companion, was going through the injured man's pockets!

The other one was talking loudly to cover up for him. "There ought to be a law against jaywalkin'!" he said irritably. "He stepped right in front of the car. How could I help smacking him?" The one who was talking had a square sort of face, with a large, wide nose, and a chin that bulged at the tip.

The woman who had dashed across the street with Ed leaped upon them now like a whirlwind. She shoved the square-faced man with her elbow, so that he almost fell from his squatting position. Then she enfolded the victim's head in her arms and wailed, "My husband! Poor George!" She glared at the other man, who had stopped his search suddenly. "What have you done to him, you—you—!"

She was slim, under thirty, dark. But Ed couldn't tell whether she was pretty or not, because of the make-up on her face.

The injured man breathed deeply, painfully. He was unconscious, of course. Ed noted once more that his face was red and blistered, as from severe sunburn.

The woman's hands explored the victim's torso, and she shouted at the motorist who still knelt beside her, looking as if he wanted to throttle her. "You've broken all his ribs!" She sobbed then: "He won't live. He won't live, I tell you! Damn you, why didn't you look where you were going!"

The one who knelt beside her seemed to control a desire to punch her in the face. He gulped, glared, and said with a pronounced lisp, "I'm thorry lady, but it wath an accident. We'll take him to the hothpital if you want."

THE WOMAN did not answer him. She bent over the victim, burying her head on his chest, and sobbing. Her shoulders, in fact her whole body, shook with the vehemence of her sobs.

A police patrol-car pulled up alongside; it contained a uniformed sergeant who was making the rounds with the driver. The sergeant approached the scene majestically through the ready lane that was opened for him by the crowd.

"Who's the driver that hit him?" he demanded. "Pick him up and get him to the hospital quick. You want him to die on your hands?"

The crowd was now watching the sergeant and the two men from the car. Probably the only one there who kept his eyes on the woman was Ed Race. In any event, he was the only one there who saw that, while she sobbed hysterically, her gloved right hand was in the injured man's lower left-hand vest pocket. Only a moment it lingered there, came out empty, and flew to the upper one on the same side. She withdrew it almost at once, clutching something, just as the sergeant tapped her on the shoulder.

"Let's get at him, lady. Crying won't do you any good. We got to get him out of here."

Still wracked by sobs, she stood up, her back to the sergeant, and covered her face with a handkerchief which she produced from under her glove.

The two men from the car stooped, lifted the victim, carried him to the auto, and deposited him in the rear seat. The sergeant ordered the driver of the prowl car, "Leave the bus here, Finnegan, and go with them to the hospital. Then bring them down to the house an' see if the lieutenant wants to hold them. I'll drive the bus back myself."

He turned just in time to see the woman slipping away into the crowd.

"Hey, lady," he shouted. "Wait a minute!"

Ed Race had seen the woman start to slip away, had watched her face as she brushed by him. She stopped now at the sergeant's call, almost touching Ed. Her body stiffened and she reeled a little, clutching Ed's arm. Ed caught her around the waist, supported her, getting the scent of a strong perfume.

Ed's keen sense caught something else, too; the woman, as she reeled against him, had slipped something into the outside pocket of his coat. She had done it so deftly, so expertly, that any other man would never have noticed it.

She recovered in a moment, took a half-step away, and turned to meet the sergeant. That officer exclaimed, "Well, for the luva Pete! Since when you been married, Gertie?"

Gertie dropped her eyes, sniffled into the handkerchief.

The sergeant seized her by the shoulder, shook her roughly. "What sort of game is this, Gertie? You just come off the Island last month after doin' ninety days out of a hundred an' twenty for jostlin' in the subway; you been reportin' to Probation every week—an' here you turn up claimin' to be married to a guy that just got conked!"

She raised her eyes sullenly, but before answering she inspected Ed Race carefully as if she wanted to remember him in the future. Then she swung on the sergeant.

"Damn you, Barnes!" she spat at him. "Why can't you lay off of me? How do you know I ain't married? Sure I am. I know his name, an' everything. He's George Lasker, steward on the *Krondam*, and he and me's been married a long time—only we kept it quiet on account he's away so much!"

Sergeant Barnes retained his grip on her shoulder. "That may be, Gertie, but just the same I'll hold on to you till we get the low-down on this business."

The patrolman on the beat had arrived on the scene by this time, and Barnes called him over. "Hold this dame," he ordered. "We'll take her in."

Gertie said, "Wait a minute, will you?" She looked at Ed Race appealingly. "Say mister, you seen the accident an' everything; how about you give me your name and address so's you can be a witness when we sue those guys in the car?"

SHE HAD a grip on Ed's sleeve now; she wasn't going to let

him go till she learned where to get him. Ed hadn't had a chance to put a hand in his pocket yet, but whatever she had placed there must be important. He had no doubt now that the two men in the car had deliberately struck down their victim to get it.

He said, "Sorry, lady, you must be mistaken. I didn't see a thing; I just got here." He was making the seven o'clock plane for Chicago in the morning, and he did not want to be held over for questioning in police-court.

Sergeant Barnes eyed him suspiciously. "Sa-y! Whaddya mean, you just got here! I saw you here when I pulled up!" He stepped closer to Ed, stared at him gloweringly. "This has the look of a phony deal all around—maybe some kind of insurance racket frame-up. I think you're in with the dame one way or another. What's your name?"

Ed sighed. The thing was getting all tangled up. "My name is Race," he said. "I'm an actor. I never saw this woman before."

Barnes leered at him. "An actor, huh? A *bad-actor*, I'll bet. Let's see what you got on you." He put out his hand to spread Ed's coat, preparatory to searching him.

Ed pushed him away. "Naughty, naughty, Sergeant! Mustn't search like that. Don't you know the rules? If you want to search someone you have to arrest him and book him first."

Barnes got ugly. "A wise guy, huh? Know all the rules, don't you? Well, see how you like this one!" He aimed a clumsy, lumbering swing at Ed's jaw. Ed blocked it easily with his left. He didn't want to get into a brawl with Barnes, and he didn't want to be searched right now, either.

Even as he blocked the blow, he saw his salvation. A squad

car swung into the curb, scattering some of the crowd who had spread out into the gutter. The brakes squealed, the door flung open, and Acting-Captain Bland of Homicide, recently promoted from Detective-sergeant, sprang out.

Bland and Barnes. Their names began with the same letter, but there the similarity ended. Barnes was a plodding precinct man who would never get beyond his present position. Bland was ten years younger, and he was going places in the department, because of his keenness and intelligence. He knew Ed Race well, had even made use of Ed's special abilities on occasion.

Ed called out to him, "Hey, Steve! Come here and take this gorilla off my hands before he breaks my neck!"

Acting-Captain Bland shoved through the crowd, growling, "Hello, Barnes. This guy is okay, only he's a little hotheaded. Don't take him too serious." Then he turned to Ed. "Every time I put my eyes on you, Race, there's trouble around."

Barnes said, "Well, Captain, if you say so, all right. But it don't look so good. Here's Gertie Sales, that's been working the subways for years, turning up and claiming to be married to a guy that got hurt in an auto accident—"

Bland shook his head. "Not hurt, Barnes—killed! He died at the hospital. That's why I'm here. It's a homicide—a double homicide."

"Double?" Barnes looked puzzled.

Bland nodded. "Finnegan, the cop you sent with those two men. I got the broadcast from downtown. After they left the hospital they jerked a gun on Finnegan, shot him in the head, and left the car. There's an alarm out for them!"

Ed had his eyes on the woman, Gertie. She did not seem unduly shocked by the news.

Bland followed his gaze, and barked at her, "You! Can you prove you're married to that man?"

She took the handkerchief away from her mouth, lowered her eyes. "Y-you can look it up in the records. George has our license somewhere."

Ed asked her, "If you're his wife you ought to know what all that red mess on his face was from?"

She nodded. "Sunburn. The *Krondam* was on a cruise, and he got two days off at Milan. He got the burn on the beach there, an' it blistered somethin' terrible. He's been treatin' it for two weeks now."

Bland looked doubtfully from Gertie to Ed. Then he said crisply to Barnes, "Hold that woman here. I want to question her some more in a minute." He took Ed Race by the arm, led him away from the others. "Look here, Race, you're a square guy. But it looks to me like you know something about this business. So, spill me what you know, or I'll have to hold you—much as I'd regret it," he added with a grin.

"Yeah," Ed exclaimed. "You'd regret it! You know damn well that this is my last night in New York. You'd laugh up your sleeve if I missed my plane for Chicago in the morning!"

HE WAS sure now, that whatever object it was that rested in his pocket it had some bearing—an important bearing—on the case. If he told Bland about it, he'd certainly have to stay over to testify in the morning. "Look here, Steve," he urged. "Would you take my word if I told you something?"

Bland nodded reluctantly. "I guess so," grudgingly. "You're straight, even if you are tricky."

"All right. I give you my word, Steve, that I never saw that man who was killed, or the woman, or the two men in the car, before in my life. I don't know them from Adam. Is that strong enough?"

Bland glowered at him. Then he sighed. "I guess so, Race. I hope I'm not making a mistake in letting you go; if I am, the inspector will be giving me hell."

Ed said, "Thanks, Steve. I appreciate it." He was already walking away. "I'll send you a postcard from Chicago."

Bland called after him worriedly, "If I should need you, will you be at your hotel tonight?"

"Yep. Till six in the morning."

Ed walked west, crossed Sixth Avenue, and entered a glittering new cafeteria a few doors beyond the corner. He did not look back, but went up to the counter, ordered a cup of coffee and a slice of butter-crumb cake, although he had eaten only a little while ago.

As he turned away with his tray, to seek a table, he grinned to himself. For there had entered, with a self-conscious appearance of nonchalance, a broad-shouldered man whom Ed immediately recognized as one of the detectives who had come with Bland in the squad car. Bland had not believed him one hundred percent.

The detective got a cup of coffee, sat at a table across the length of the cafeteria from the spot Ed had chosen.

DEATH'S SPOTLIGHT

Ed finished his coffee, leaving most of the cake, and rose. Instead of leaving, he made his way toward the rear, and entered the men's wash-room. There was nobody else here at the moment, and he hastily brought out from his pocket the object that the woman had dropped into it.

It was a flat, brass key-check, made to fit into some sort of slot. Upon its face was the lettering:

Times Square Self-Service Checking System

Do not lose this key.

Number 7

Ed recalled the steel lockers in the Times Square subway station. It was an ingenious checking room which did not require an attendant. One inserted a dime in the slot of whichever box he chose, and the door opened automatically. He put his parcel in, closed the door, and the key was delivered to him through a slot. When he returned for his parcel, he inserted the key in the slot, the locker opened, and he took his parcel out.

Ed slipped the brass check back in his pocket just as the washroom door opened to admit a thin, dried-up, undersized man with shifty eyes. Ed had seen this one come into the cafeteria with two others right after the detective, but he had paid no more than cursory attention to the three of them.

The thin man was no sooner inside the door than he produced a gun from his side pocket, leveled it at Ed. His lips, which were very thin and bloodless, uttered curt, clipped words:

"Give me that brass check, bo, or get burned down!"

His cold eyes were on Ed's pocket, where his hand still held the check. Ed saw that the muzzle of the gun was pointed unwaveringly at his middle.

He shrugged, slowly withdrew his hand, holding the check. "You want it pretty bad, don't you?"

"Never mind the talk," the thin man snarled. "Give it here!"

Ed said, "Here!" and flipped it in the air toward the other man. Involuntarily, the thin man put out his hand to catch it. It's impossible for anyone to try to catch something in the air and, at the same time, hold a bead on another man. The gunman's eyes wavered toward the brass check sailing in the air.

And in that instant, Ed's hand, moving in a continuous, swift blur of action, had drawn his own forty-five from the shoulder holster.

The thin man's gun wavered a few inches. He now frantically swung it back toward Ed, letting the key-check tinkle on the floor. But the barrel of Ed's revolver connected with that chin with a nasty thud. All the thin man's muscles seemed to loosen up, and he wilted, his hand opening nervelessly to allow the gun to drop.

ED CAUGHT the gun in the air, lest it explode when it hit the floor. He let the man slump down, however, and remain inert. He placed the gun beside the unconscious man, after wiping his own prints off it. Then he picked up the check, and walked calmly out of the washroom.

He paid his fifteen cents at the cashier's desk, stepped out into the street. He was conscious of the detective following him out, and he also noted that the two men who had come in with the thin one had, after a moment of indecision, also risen. One of them came after him, out to the street, while the other went back to the washroom.

Ed proceeded leisurely across Forty-Second Street to Times Square, conscious of the procession behind him. He was a little thankful for the detective at his immediate rear. It reduced the danger of a bullet in the back.

Ed felt a little safer as he pushed through to the subway entrance, walked down to the lower level. He passed the lockers to one of which he held the key. They stood against a wall near the entrance. Number seven—what did it contain? Ed was sorely tempted to open it right then; but he caught a glimpse of the detective who was trailing him, and the other two men— the second had evidently caught up with the first, and they both looked mad as hornets. They were just coming down the stairs.

Ed put a nickel in the turnstile machine, and passed through, walked down to the south-bound platform. A train was just roaring in. Ed walked to the south end of the platform, and waited there. He half-turned, saw the detective and the other two a little beyond him. He turned away quickly, as if he had not noticed them, and when the train pulled in and the doors opened, he stepped in.

Out of the corner of his eye he saw his three trailers enter another car of the train, further back. He waited a moment till the doors started to close, then slipped out, back on to the platform. The doors slid to, and he had a glimpse of the detective's bewildered expression staring out at him as the train flashed past. In the next car he saw the other two, also glaring at him.

He grinned, strode upstairs, and went boldly to the automatic lockers. He inserted the key in number seven, and the door swung open. He peered inside, and uttered an involuntary gasp of amazement. The dark, shadowy interior of the locker revealed nothing. Empty!

It was hard to believe that men had committed murder to get a key to an empty locker. He lit a match, held it so that the light shone on the inside. And then he saw it.

It was just a square piece of printed cardboard, and it lay in the corner where it had been invisible at first. He reached in and picked it up, and examined it. It was a baggage-check for one piece of luggage checked at the Pennsylvania Station.

Ed wanted to laugh. This would have been funny if it hadn't been for what went before. He slammed the door of the locker shut, and went up to the street. He could see where he wouldn't get much sleep tonight if he followed the thing up. But he could no more have dropped the business there than a drug addict can rid himself of the craving for drugs.

He hailed a cab and said, "Pennsylvania Station."

At the station parcel-room Ed presented the check, and in a moment the attendant passed over the counter a small Boston bag. "Twenty cents due on it," he announced. "Two days overtime."

Ed took the bag into the waiting room, sat down, and tried it. It was locked. He produced from his vest pocket a short length of thin but strong steel. He inserted one end of this under the lock and pried with it. The cheap lock was made for show rather than protection, and it gave under the pressure, the bag springing open.

The bag contained a dirty shirt, two dirty pair of socks, three soiled handkerchiefs, a bottle of medicine and a pint jar of salve. It also contained a seaman's book. The book was made out in the name of George Lasker, and the picture was a good likeness of the man who had been run down by the car.

Inside the seaman's book there were several folded papers of a personal nature—a couple of bills for dentist work in Rotterdam, a receipt for head-tax which Lasker paid in order to be allowed to leave his boat in New York for five days, and a marriage license dated one month ago, apparently when his ship had last visited New York. The marriage license was duly made out in the name of George Lasker and Gertie Sales.

ED FOUND nothing else. There wasn't enough to warrant murder. He half expected to find another baggage check, or something that would take him on another chase, but there was nothing.

The medicine bottle contained an amber-colored liquid, and bore the label of a Dutch pharmacist in Amsterdam. The jar of salve came from England, and read:

Marsh's Calamine Unguent—for relief of severe sunburn.

The salve had no odor at all, and the medicine smelled strongly of vinegar. Gertie had been right on every count. But she had certainly not seemed to be telling the truth.

Ed got the bag packed again, closed it as best he could, and went out into the street. He got in a cab and ordered, "Longmont Hotel—on Forty-eighth."

At the hotel, Ed got his key at the desk, went up to the twelfth floor in the elevator, carrying Lasker's bag under his arm so as not to spill the contents.

He opened the door of his room, kicked it shut after entering, and felt for the light switch. When he snapped it on he blinked his eyes at the sight that confronted him. Tied on the bed was the broad-shouldered detective who had followed him down to the Times Square subway station. On the two chairs in the room sat two other men. They were the two motorists who had run down Lasker. There was an alarm out for them, but it didn't seem to bother them much. They both had guns, and the guns had been directed at the doorway, so that when Ed entered he was covered. They had been waiting for him in the dark.

The detective was gagged, and he was making violent noises through the towel that had been tied around his mouth.

The man with the square face rose, grinning wickedly. His eyes were on the bag under Ed's arm, and his face bore a look of greedy satisfaction.

"Hello," Ed said mildly. "How did you boys all get here?"

Square-face said nothing. But the other one piped up: "Very thimple. When our two men lotht you in the thubway, they followed thith detective, and where should he go, but up here? Tho our men came in after him and tied him. Then they thent for uth to do the dirty work. You ought to thank uth for tying him up—he wath doing thomething very wrong; he wath thearching your room."

The square-faced one growled to his companion, "Lay off the talk, Slemp." His eyes were still on Ed. He ordered curtly, "Give us that bag!"

88

Ed held it out to him. "It's a pleasure. Is this what all the shooting's been about?"

Square-face didn't bother to answer. Instead he directed out of the corner of his mouth, "Take it, Slemp."

Slemp took the bag out of Ed's hands, exclaimed, "He'th opened it, Mickey. The lock ith buthted!" He dumped the contents on the bed close to the detective's legs, said sadly, "Nothing in here, Mickey."

Mickey snarled at Ed, "Give us what you took out of there, boy. And give it quick!" The gun in his hand moved forward an inch toward Ed's middle.

"Everything is in the bag the way I found it," Ed told him. "I didn't take a thing out of it. Somebody must have been giving you boys a joyride."

Mickey continued to watch Ed. He asked Slemp, "You sure that's Lasker's bag?"

"Yeth. Here are hith papers; and here ith the medicine he uthed for hith thunburn. It'th Lathher'th, all right."

Mickey started to grin thinly, dangerously. "Trying to get away with something, huh? Well, boy, last chance—do you come across?"

Ed was becoming annoyed. He didn't like the muzzle of that gun yawning at his stomach.

"If you'll tell me what I'm supposed to have—?" he began.

"Listen," Mickey interrupted savagely, "you must be awful dumb if you think you can kid us out of those stones. There's two men dead already—another one would make no difference to us—at all. Well?"

"Nope," Slemp said cheerfully. "It would be great fun to knock you off, mithter. You better give uth thothe four diamondth while you're thtill alive."

Ed sighed. "All right, you win." They'd never be convinced that Ed didn't have the diamonds. "I've got them," Ed lied. "They're tied around my garter."

Mickey's eyes lit with triumph. "Give us!"

Ed bent over, reached toward his trouser-leg to pull it up.

"I gueth you are pretty dumb after all, mithter," Slemp remarked. "Did you figure to get away with thothe thtoneth?"

ED DIDN'T answer. He knew two guns were trained on him. In a moment, when it was discovered that he was bluffing, one or both of these guns would vomit death at him.

As he bent over, his coat came open, the handle of the big forty-five in his shoulder holster sagged low. And Ed did now what he had often done on the stage without the same grim necessity to succeed. He appeared to slip as he bent, but instead of recovering his balance, he continued the motion, going into a complete somersault. He had done that somersault on the stage every night for six years, coming out of it with a gun in his hand, and shooting a target no larger than a silver dollar, thirty feet away. Now he had human targets.

Two guns blazed at him, the room was filled with reverberating gunfire. But his somersault had carried him just past the foot of the bed, and the slugs from those guns clanged into the brass bedstead. Ed's revolver was in his hand almost with the echo of the first shots. He fired twice—once at Slemp, once at Mickey—and got slowly to his feet.

Slemp was lying half across the bed, blood from the hole in his head staining the detective's trousers a deep red. Mickey had been pushed back against the wall by the force of the heavy slug that had caught him in the right shoulder. His face was very white, and he slid down to the floor, letting the gun drop from nerveless fingers.

Ed grinned at the detective, who looked somewhat green in the gills. He reached over and untied the gag. There was the sound of excited voices in the corridor outside—the shots had been plenty loud.

The detective gasped, when his mouth was free, "Boy! That was some shooting!" His voice was almost drowned by the jangling of the telephone. "I'm Colter, of Homicide," he explained, looking sheepish. "I called Bland when you tricked me in the subway, an' he told me to come up here an' wait for you."

Ed had left him tied, crossed over and picked up the 'phone. Acting-Captain Bland's voice came sputtering over the wire. "Hello! Colter! Why the hell did you take so long answering? Hasn't Race come in yet? I got to see him!"

Ed said into the 'phone, "This isn't Colter, Steve. This is Ed Race."

There was a moment of embarrassed silence at the other end. Then, explosively, "Listen, Race, you pulled a fast one on me. I got Gertie to talk down here. She says she slipped a brass check in your pocket. It's supposed to be for some check room in the city, she don't know where. Lasker smuggled four diamonds in somehow on the boat, working with a smuggling clique here in the city. They paid for the stones in advance, and then he was going to double-cross them. He was supposed to meet Gertie and they was going to blow with thirty thousand dollars' worth of stones! If they're recovered now, the government will pay a reward of twenty-five percent!"

Ed whistled. Someone was trying the door tentatively from the corridor. Ed covered the mouthpiece, called out, "It's all right. I'll open up in a minute." He spoke into the receiver again. "Better come up here, Steve. I think I can introduce you to that smuggling clique. But those diamonds—I think they're a fairy tale."

"I'll be over," said Bland, "in about four minutes. Say, while I think of it—here's something funny. The Medical Examiner's right here, and he says Lasker didn't have sunburn at all. Those blisters were brought about by having tincture of cantharides applied to his face."

Ed gripped the 'phone. "What? Wait a minute! Hold on, Steve!" He put the 'phone down, rushed to the bed, unceremoniously pushed the dead Slemp to the floor, and snatched up the bottle of amber colored liquid, and the jar of salve. On the way back to the 'phone he unlocked the door to admit the house-detective and a uniformed patrolman who pushed in gazing about the room in wonder.

Ed said to them, "Everything's okay. I have headquarters on the wire now. Untie him." He motioned toward the bed, then reached for the 'phone once more.

"Hey, Steve! Ask the M.E. what this tincture of cantharides smells like. Does it smelt of vinegar?"

After a moment the answer came. "Yep. It blisters you up. Why?"

"This Lasker put it on his face on purpose, so's the Customs men would think he had sunburn. Then they wouldn't suspect a nice big jar of salve, would they?"

WHILE HE talked he had twisted open the lid of the jar, dug his fingers into the white substance. Colter was untied now, and he and the others crowded around while Ed pulled out, one after the other, four diamonds, each one almost the size of a dime in diameter.

He grinned into the telephone, winked at Colter. "Okay, Steve. Come on up. I'll introduce you to the diamonds, too!"

BILLED FOR DEATH!

THE CONDUCTOR of the milk-train opened the door, letting in a swirl of night wind and cinders. "Trout City," he called. "Show your tickets, please. Trout City." The train started to slow up; the conductor fixed the door open and stood for a moment in the vestibule.

Ed Race started to get up from the last seat in the day-coach, grateful that he had arrived here at last. Down the aisle a fat man snored, lurching forward in his seat with the halted momentum of the train. But Ed Race's eyes were fixed on the little, wizened man who was seated next to the fat sleeper. He saw, in the flash of an instant, one thin, claw-like hand dart toward the fat man's coat; saw that hand flash out again, holding a wallet; and then the back of the seat hid the hand and its contents. The little man feigned a yawn, stretched, got up and transferred to a seat just behind his stout, still sleeping victim.

The fat man woke up. His hand went at once to his breast pocket. His eyes opened wider. He grumbled something and started searching the floor. The little pickpocket glanced behind him, saw Ed looking at him, and flushed guiltily. Ed got up.

So did the little dip. He lunged past the conductor, just as the train grumbled to a jerky stop, with Ed behind him, yelling at him to stop. But the little man paid no attention. He leaped down and started running in the shadows across the station platform.

Behind Ed Race pandemonium broke loose in the car. The fat man, thoroughly aroused, was lumbering down the aisle, shouting, "Get those crooks!" The conductor was adding his voice to the shouts and rapidly-flung questions of the other passengers.

Ed threw back an annoyed glance and jumped down from the car platform to the plank flooring of the station.

This wasn't exactly the way Ed Race had planned to arrive in Trout City. His specialty was a juggling act with the Midwest Vaudeville Circuit—"The Masked Marksman," was his billing— and Ed could do things with those six forty-five revolvers that weren't in any of the books. Everything would have been fine if Jake Landor, boss of the vaudeville circuit, had not discovered that Ed's sideline was dabbling in crime. He had a license in a dozen states to operate as a private detective. When Jake Landor found that out, he sent Ed a telegram at Evansville.

Catch midnight for Trout City stop our manager there in trouble stop take guns stop spare no expense to clean it up.
Landor.

Ed had grabbed the first train, and now here he was. But instead of getting off in a leisurely fashion, he found himself in this pickpocket chase. Added to that, he was also accused by the bawling fat man.

Ed didn't get very far in that race across the platform. He skidded to a fast stop, warned by some sixth sense that hell was going to cut loose. He jumped back onto the car and hugged the wall of the platform.

For in the darkness just beyond the station lights there burst the nasty chatter of an automatic rifle. The quick staccato was accompanied by the whine of steel-jacketed slugs which smashed into the body of the fleeing pickpocket.

His body hurtled through the air, flung back by the bullet impact, then fell limply to the wooden boards of the platform. He jerked once or twice, then was still.

AT ONCE the barking of the automatic rifle ceased. From somewhere out in the darkness beyond the lights of the station there was the sound of an automobile motor being raced, of tires crunching on gravel, of a car speeding away.

For a moment all was silent, in weird startling contrast to the wicked racket of a second ago. Then men came running out of the waiting room of the station; a police siren shrilled. Everybody was moving, shouting—everybody but the little pickpocket, who would never move any more.

Ed Race looked thoughtful as he leaped to the platform and picked up one of the automatic rifle slugs which had rebounded from the steel side of the car.

If it hadn't been for the pickpocket's attempted escape, Ed would have been the first one to get off the train. He would have received that hail of lead and he would now be lying on the platform where, instead, the little man lay.

The killers, whoever they were, could never have known that the pickpocket would get off here, because the little fellow hadn't expected to have to get off himself. Ed's arrival could have been

known to them—telegrams are not exactly private. Ed was convinced that the party had been staged for his benefit.

But why?

He joined the group around the dead man, when he heard the irate voice of the bald-headed man from inside the car, shouting, "Get that other crook that tried to run away with him. They were working together. Don't let him get away!"

Ed looked up at the lighted windows of the car he had just left, saw the conductor and the bald-headed man coming down the aisle toward the vestibule. If he stayed here he'd have a lot of explaining to do, and he'd certainly be held for questioning as an eye-witness of the killing. Ed Race had no desire to be held in jail in a strange town—especially in a town where there seemed to be someone highly interested in his demise.

As the conductor and the bald-headed man stepped into the vestibule, Ed bent low, walked under the couplings between the coaches and emerged on the other side of the train.

He walked rapidly toward the locomotive, then, when he was almost abreast of it he cut sharply across the tracks and disappeared into one of the side streets leading from the station.

At a corner cab-stand Ed got into the one decrepit-looking hack and said to the driver, "Trout City Theater."

Jake Landor's wire had been very uninformative! It hadn't given the theater manager's name, nor had it stated the kind of trouble he was in. The night watchman at the theater would give Ed the manager's name and address, Ed knew.

After a few moments Ed looked up at the darkened facade of the Trout City Theater, before which they had stopped. He got out, paid the driver and saw him grind away. Then he walked up to the padlocked glass doors that spread across the lobby, and peered into opaque darkness beyond. His hand grasped the set of skeleton keys in his pocket. Then suddenly, he stepped back into the shadows.

Another cab was slowing up outside. He nudged with his left arm at the forty-five in the shoulder clip, so as to bring the butt slightly forward. It was one of the six that he used in his juggling act. He carried it in preference to a smaller, perhaps handier gun, because he was used to the heft of it.

BILLED FOR DEATH!

THE CAB pulled up ten or fifteen feet from the theater entrance, and a dumpy, roly-poly man got out and paid off the driver. He shoved his hat far back on a glistening, sweat-beaded forehead, and looked around as if he were seeking someone who was supposed to be there.

The man's coat collar was half turned up, and his shirt, hastily put on, bagged out over his paunch.

Ed's eyes swept the street, but he saw no one else. He started to come out of his place of retirement, but edged back into the shadow when he observed two men rounding the opposite corner. These men walked slowly but purposely, and each had a hand in his coat pocket.

The hastily-dressed, stout man seemed not to have noticed these two. He walked under the marquee of the theater. He must have discerned the dark blob which Ed made in the shadows, for he took a slow step nearer. Then he stopped and called out anxiously in a low, hoarse whisper: "Mr. Race? It's all right, Mr. Race, I'm Hadley—the manager."

Ed didn't answer him. He was busy watching the two men across the street. They were walking slowly now, their eyes on the theater, hands still in their pockets. Up and down the avenue there was no sign of life except for the lights of an all-night coffee-pot down the middle of the next block. Two o'clock in the morning is a quiet time in a small town.

Hadley also must have seen those two men across the street, but he went on talking nervously.

Ed kept his eyes on the two men and asked Hadley, "How'd you know I'd be here?"

Hadley started to beam with satisfaction. "Say, Mr. Race, I'm glad it's you; I was that upset. I just got a telegram from Mr. Landor in Chicago, saying he'd sent you a wire, but had forgotten to give my name, so you'd probably come to the theater. Want to see—"

He took a crumpled yellow form from his pocket, extended it toward Ed, but did not come any closer. Neither did he finish his question. For the two men across the street had gone into action the moment that he held out the yellow blank.

Their hands came from their pockets, and each one had a gun.

Ed swung sideways, snaking out his revolver with a motion so swift that his draw was completed before those guns across the street could belch their lead.

Even as he fired, almost simultaneously with the two on the opposite side, he knew that they were not aiming at Hadley, but at himself. The bark of their automatics, mingling with the deep-throated shattering reports of Ed Race's forty-five, blasted sudden sound the length of the avenue.

The aim of the two gunmen was far from good. Their slugs screeched on the sidewalk paving, clanged against the steel-enclosed ticket booth which stood just before the theater entrance, and smashed the glass of the wide lobby doors. None of them found Ed Race.

Ed, on the other hand, fired only twice; and as if by a miracle the noise and thunder of the shooting ceased. The two gunmen sprawled on the street.

Ed returned the forty-five to its clip, bounded over to where Hadley had dropped to his knees, white-faced.

Men were running toward them from the coffee-pot down the avenue, and somewhere a policeman was blowing a whistle. Ed seized Hadley by the arm, jerked him up to his feet.

There was no chance of escaping in either direction, and Ed didn't want to be held by the police now, any more than he had wanted it before. Hadley was moaning and shaking in panic.

Ed grabbed his shoulder. "Have you got the keys to the theater?"

Hadley shook his head. "I l-left t-them home!" he stammered.

One of the full-length glass doors was shattered by the gunfire, leaving jagged edges. He took out his revolver, slapped off the sharp pieces and forced the shivering manager in ahead of him.

They were in shadow, and the men who were running toward the scene from down the street couldn't see them. Within the lobby it was dark. Ed kept his grip on Hadley's arm. "Lead the way inside. We'll get out the side door."

The manager walked ahead through the darkened theater, with Race following.

FROM OUTSIDE there came a wild clamor of excited people, mingled with the blasts of police whistles and the sirens of radio patrol cars. Ed reflected that if the fracas at the station hadn't completely awakened the town, this surely had. So far he had been shot at, nearly shot at, almost arrested; and he was still in the dark as to what it was all about. Mentally he cursed Jake Landor for his thriftiness in that telegram—just a few more words would have given him the whole setup so that he could act with some degree of intelligence.

Hadley brought him down the side aisle to an alley door, manipulated the lever that locked it, and swung it open. A blast of cold air drove into their faces, and they stepped out just as the sound of heavy footsteps, curses and shouts, came from the lobby. The officers had found the broken door, and come through.

Ed swung the big door shut behind them. The wind whistled down the alley. "W-what'll we do now?" Hadley trembled. "W-we c-can't get away with that crowd up in front."

"Who said so?" Ed demanded. He pushed the other ahead of him till they got to the alley mouth. Where there had been, five minutes ago, nobody but Ed and Hadley and the two gunmen, there were now almost a hundred persons herding around on the sidewalk in front of the theater and across the street where the two bodies lay.

A number of police cars were pulled up at the curb, and uniformed men were busy keeping the crowd in check.

Ed followed Hadley out into the street, where they mingled with the others. No one noticed them.

Ed still kept his grip on the manager's arm, and whispered, "We just got here, get it? You want to know what it's all about. Come on over and ask the cops." He started Hadley over to cross the street.

A tall officer with white hair and wise eyes was in charge there. He swung around as they pushed through to the little circle about the two gunmen's bodies.

"Hullo, Hadley. This is a hell of a note. Right in front of your theater, too. Know anything about it?"

Hadley gulped, stiffened under Ed's grip, and said, "Not a thing, Captain Manners. This is terrible. They've smashed the glass in my doors. Who are they?"

Manners shrugged. "Nothing on them to show." He gazed down somberly at the two corpses. "Whoever shot them was an ace—got them both right through the heart, while they were peppering away at him." He swung around, saw Ed Race, and lifted his brows. "Friend of yours, Hadley?"

Hadley said quickly, "Yes, yes. This is Mr. Race, one of the actors on our circuit. Mr. Race, Captain Manners of the Trout City Police Department."

Manners eyed Ed up and down. "Race, eh? I seem to have heard that name somewhere. When did you get in town, Mr. Race?" He went on without giving Ed a chance to reply, "You didn't get in on the milk train, by any chance, did you? There was a ruckus over at the station a while ago when the milk train came in. A chap got shot up."

Ed shrugged. "We wouldn't know about that, Captain."

Just then a plainclothes man came around the corner, carrying a sub-machine gun. He saluted Captain Manners and said, "We found this in a sedan parked around the corner, sir. Must belong to these two birds. I guess it's the one that was used at the station. The drum is empty, and there's no more drums in the car. So I guess they figured they'd use their rods on this job."

Manners reached excitedly for the gun. Ed nudged the theater manager, urged him out of the crowd. They were forgotten in the general excitement about the newly-found machine gun.

ED GUIDED Hadley down the street, hailed a cab, pushed

Hadley into it and got in after him. "Give him your address," he ordered the theater manager.

Hadley was wiping sweat from his forehead with a soiled handkerchief. He gasped out, "Forty-two, Grove Street."

The cab passed the crowd in front of the theatre, and continued up the main street. They drove for seven or eight blocks along the avenue, then turned left, and pulled up before a comfortable-looking, two story and attic frame house.

Ed got to the sidewalk, paid for the ride, then he and Hadley started across the well-kept lawn.

There was a light in the downstairs window on the ground floor, and none in any other part of the house except in a small window of the attic.

At the door, Hadley felt in his pocket, murmured apologetically, "Those damn keys! I forgot them." He put his finger on the button and rang the bell. "I live here alone," he explained, "with my housekeeper and my niece. It's about my niece—"

He was interrupted by the opening of the front door. A scrawny woman in a bathrobe admitted them. She was a bleached blonde, and her finger-waved hair was done up in a net.

She looked suspiciously at Ed, and stood aside for them to enter. Hadley led the way into the living room which was at the front, and said hospitably, "Sit down, Mr. Race, sit down. I'll have Emma get you a drink."

Ed sat down in an easy chair, and looked around the room. He noted that beside the door which opened from the hall, there was another, now closed, leading to the rear.

Hadley went out, and Ed heard him whispering to the

woman, Emma, in the hall. He couldn't catch the words, but the woman's voice was insistent, and Hadley's was worried. In a few moments, Hadley came back into the room. He stood before Ed, trying to smile but not making a very good job of it.

"This business, Mr. Race, is making a wreck out of me. It was damn good of Jake Landor to send you out here. I've been beside myself for the last three days."

Ed stood up, walked to the window, and looked out into the street, then turned back and faced the theater manager.

"Look, Mr. Hadley," he said. "Never mind whom you've been beside for the last three days. See if you can get down to brass tacks and tell me what this is all about. Why does Jake Landor send me a crazy telegram that drags me out here on the milk train, and why does a poor punk get all perforated by machine-gun bullets on account of being mistaken for me? Also, why do I get shot at the minute you arrive in front of the Trout City Theater? In short, Mr. Hadley, you take a good long breath and tell me what this is all about!"

Hadley's eyes dropped before Ed's angry gaze. "It's like this, Mr. Race, just like I started to tell you. It's about my niece. I don't know if Jake Landor told you in the telegram, but she's been kidnapped! Kidnapped three days ago, and I had to pay ten thousand dollars in cash!"

Ed Race's eyes narrowed. "So then what happened—didn't you get her back?"

Hadley shook his head. "No, Mr. Race, they haven't sent her back. They're not going to send her back, unless I pay them another ten thousand dollars. I got a telephone call this morning, from the same man who called me before. He said he knew I could raise the other ten, and that if I didn't they'd kill Alice!"

"Can you raise the other ten?" Ed asked him.

"I don't know. I haven't got any money of my own. The way I got the other ten, I wired Jake Landor, and he authorized me to borrow it from the Midwest Circuit funds that I have on deposit here in Trout City. Those damn kidnapers must know all about our business, because there's just another ten thousand on deposit here now, and they figure I can borrow that, too."

ED GRINNED. "So they look up your bank balance before they snatch you, these days?" He walked up and down the room and saw, from the corner of his eyes, the rear door open a fraction of an inch.

He stood sideways to the door. He said very loudly, "Well, why didn't you wire Jake Landor again and borrow the other ten thousand?"

"I did, Mr. Race. And Landor sent me the telegram saying that you would be over to see what it was all about."

"Did you tell anyone I was coming?"

"We-ell, I guess my housekeeper knew about it."

"How long has she been with you?"

"Oh, three or four years—ever since my wife died."

Ed was only half listening. He sidled up to the door, stole a glance at Hadley. The theater manager was gazing nervously out through the open door to the hallway, and Ed, following his gaze, caught a faint hint of motion out there in the darkness.

The door near which Ed stood had stopped moving, but a

faint whistling was audible from behind it, as if someone was attempting to hold his breath, but not entirely succeeding.

Ed Race suddenly stretched out his left hand, seized the door-knob and wrenched it open. The man who had been standing behind the door, stumbled into the room, off balance. He was a short, stocky man with a sharp nose and high cheekbones. He wore gray spats and gray gloves, and in his gloved right hand there was an automatic which he swung toward Ed.

Hadley's eyes were wide open. He cried out, "Buxton! What—"

The man in the spats paid no attention to Hadley. His eyes, and the gun in his hand, were fixed on Ed.

But Ed Race acted with the same lightning swiftness that characterized all his motions on the stage. The heavy forty-five came leaping out of his shoulder holster into his hand, almost like a live thing. It arced viciously and there was a crunch of bone as the barrel flashed down against the gunman's wrist. The automatic which had been coming up to a level with Ed's chest fell from the man's grip.

Buxton was holding his right wrist in his left hand and groaning with pain.

Hadley was standing about five or six feet from them. His face was gray; his mouth open but he seemed to have become incapable of speech.

Ed kicked Buxton's automatic over into a corner of the room, and holstered his own gun. He asked pleasantly, "Is Mr. Buxton a very good friend of yours, Mr. Hadley?"

Hadley didn't seem to know what to do with his hands or his

feet. He finally managed to get his mouth closed, then opened it again and gulped: "No—uh—that is—yes. Yes, sure he's a friend of mine. I mean—he's here on business."

Buxton seemed to be in great pain. He backed away toward an easy chair in the corner, and dropped into it, still nursing his injured hand. "Damn it, I think a bone is busted," he muttered.

Ed clucked sympathetically, "I'm awful sorry I had to get so rough, pal, but you know how it is when someone comes at you with a gun. If I had known you were a friend of Mr. Hadley's—"

Ed was looking at the injured man when he heard Hadley's voice, shrill and desperate, behind him, "Stand still, Race. If you move I'll kill you!"

Ed stood still. He recognized that tone. He could imagine the gun shaking in Hadley's trembling hand. He said, "Okay, Hadley. Take it easy with the gun. Those things go off easy." He didn't move his body, but he turned his head slightly, saw that Hadley was standing in the corner holding the automatic which he had kicked over there.

BUXTON WAS grinning. He started to get up out of the chair. "Good stuff, Hadley. You're learning fast!" He took a step toward Ed. "My left hand is still good. Hold that gun on him, while I take one good smack at him."

He raised his left fist for a chopping blow at Ed's face. "You'll take it and like it—or maybe you'd like a slug in the back better!"

Ed tensed. He was on his toes now, getting set to clinch with Buxton, to chance a shot from Hadley's gun.

But at that moment, the irate voice of the housekeeper shrilled from the hall doorway. "Stop it, you fool, stop it!" She came into the room, her hands on her hips, glaring at Buxton. "Is that all you have to do when you're in a spot like this? Why don't you use your head? There's been shooting here, the cops may come! Do you want them to find us here like this?" She jerked her head at Ed Race, "Get him upstairs out of the way. Snap it up!"

Buxton lowered his hands, backed away from Ed, snarling, "I'll give that guy a work-out before I'm through with him."

He circled around Ed, crossed the room to where Hadley stood. "Give me that gun," he growled, "I'll take care of him."

Ed had pivoted slowly with Buxton, as he moved across the room, so that he was now facing the woman and the two men. He said, "Listen, are we all crazy, or is it just me that's nuts? It looks like nobody in this town loves me. Everybody goes for me on sight!"

His eyes were on Buxton and Hadley. Hadley was standing immovable, with his arm outstretched, the automatic gripped awkwardly in his hand, and pointing directly at Ed.

Buxton was close to Hadley now. He said sharply, "Give that to a guy who knows how to use it!"

Hadley stuttered. "T-take it!" He took his finger off the trigger, and extended the automatic to Buxton, still keeping it pointed at Ed. Buxton put his left hand out and took the weapon. And in that instant Ed Race acted.

He dropped to one knee at the same time that his hand flashed to his arm-pit holster. His heavy forty-five seemed to have appeared as if by magic.

Buxton was handicapped by having to use his left hand.

Before he got his finger wrapped around the trigger, Ed's big revolver was pointed squarely at him. Ed rapped out, "Drop it, Buxton!"

Buxton's reaction was instinctive. His hand opened and let the automatic drop to the carpet. Ed glanced down at it, looked up at Buxton and grinned. "I'm what they call a prize sap. I let him hold me up with an automatic, and he didn't even know enough to take off the safety! Maybe now you'll tell me who's who in this story. It looks like Mr. Hadley has a lot of explaining to do."

That was as far as Ed got.

For the moment, he had forgotten the housekeeper. Now he was made painfully aware of her presence. Something like a ton of wildcats smashed into him, bore him backwards. Finger nails tore at his eyes, missed, and raked his cheeks. Like a snarling, furious she-panther, the housekeeper clawed at him, shrieking to the others, "Get him! Get him quick!"

Ed saw Buxton stoop for the automatic. He tried to shove the woman away from him, and swing his gun back in that direction, but she suddenly wrapped both arms around his own right arm, crushed it close to her thin breasts, and dragged it downward.

Ed got a grip on her hair with his free hand, and yanked. She uttered a cry of pain, and her head jerked back. Her grip on his arm relaxed, and in a moment he would have had it free.

But Buxton had already picked up the automatic, and was across the room in a single leap. He leaned over the woman, holding the gun in his left hand, and thrust the gun against the side of Ed's head. "Let go of the woman and the cannon," he said. "The safety is off this time!"

110

Ed sighed. He let go of the woman's hair, dropped the revolver and straightened up. He shrugged. "Well, that's the way it is— some days you can't make any headway at all."

THE WOMAN got to her feet unsteadily. She was breathing hard, her breasts rising and falling quickly. "Take him upstairs!" she said. "Get him out of here, quick." She stooped, picked up Ed's revolver and waved it impatiently. "Snap it up!"

Hadley, who had shrunk back into the corner when the gun-play threatened, now came across the room. "Yes, yes," he urged. "Then we can talk over what to do."

Buxton nudged Ed with the automatic. "Get going, guy."

Ed obeyed, turned toward the door. Buxton looked too eager to squeeze the trigger of the automatic.

The woman preceded him, turned on the hall light. Then she led the way up the carpeted stairs. Ed followed her, and Buxton came after him, with the automatic pressed close up against Ed's spine. Buxton called back to Hadley who was standing in the doorway of the living room, "Stay down there, you! If anybody comes to ask about that shot that was fired, tell them they were nuts."

Hadley called up after them, "Be careful will you, Buxton? Don't hurt him bad. We might need him to get Landor to shell out the other ten thousand!"

They were at the top of the flights of stairs now. Buxton growled down to Hadley, "Never mind the advice. You just do what you're told!"

The housekeeper, without saying a word, led the way along the upper corridor, and then up another flight of narrow stairs.

The attic was divided into a narrow hall and two small rooms. The woman stopped before the door of the second room. Ed noted that both doors were secured with padlocks on the outside. He watched while the woman got the door open, and then he walked in after her, urged by Buxton's gun.

The room was small. There was not a stick of furniture in it. The only light came from an electric bulb out in the hallway. High up in the sloping attic roof there was a small window with panes of glazed glass.

Ed looked around, turned to Buxton who had remained at the door. His face was expressionless. "How about a chair?" he asked. "The floor is kind of inconvenient to sit on."

Buxton's face was screwed into a snarl. He glanced down to his right hand, which was already swollen to almost twice its normal size, then up again at Ed. "When I get through with you," he said, "you'll be damn lucky if you're able to sit up on the floor!"

The housekeeper was standing near the door, holding Ed's revolver. "Listen, Buxton," she protested, "why start—?"

"Can it!" Buxton snarled at her. "This guy busted my hand, and I'm going to bust his map!"

The woman raised the revolver, pointed it at Ed. "Okay, then. This cannon ought to hold him quiet while you work on him."

Buxton's eyes narrowed, and his lips spread in a thin smile. "What a pleasure!" he exclaimed. He took a step toward Ed, raised the automatic. "Did you ever have your face raked by a gun-barrel?" he asked softly.

Ed said earnestly, "See here, Buxton, why don't you act your age? You'll only get me sore—"

He stopped.

From the next room there had come a low moaning sound. It was followed by a wet sort of cough, and then the moan was repeated. A childish voice shrilled weakly, "It's dark in here. I'm afraid!"

THE HOUSEKEEPER said, "It's the kid. She must have come out of the ether." Buxton's eyes were still viciously on Ed. "To hell with her!" He brought down the gun with a slashing stroke, that cut open Ed's cheek to the bone. Ed staggered backwards. The pain in his cheek was intense. Blood dribbled down to his coat. His face felt numb, and he started to get dizzy.

He shook his head and crouched, bending at the knees. He would have jumped at Buxton if the woman's shrill voice had not come to him. "Take it easy, mister. I can shoot this cannon of yours fine." She chuckled. "You just stand there and take it, mister!"

Buxton raised the gun again. Ed said slowly, "I don't like it, and I'm not going to take it." He shot forward like a catapult, head low, and caught Buxton in the groin with his shoulder.

Buxton doubled up, uttering a shriek of agony.

They both sprawled on the floor, Buxton clutching at his abdomen, his breath coming through his teeth in a wheeze of agony. They had made a fair amount of noise, and from the next room there came once more the childish voice, raised in terror, "I'm afraid!"

Ed rolled over after hitting Buxton. He lurched to his knees and gripped Buxton's left wrist, whose hand still held the automatic.

The woman had been bewildered by the swift action. Now, when she saw Buxton helpless she stepped in, gripping the big revolver firmly. Her eyes were gray and flat-looking, and her knuckles were white on the stock as she swept the revolver out toward Ed. She said, "Get up, you—" And she stopped abruptly.

From below came the insistent, clamorous ringing of the doorbell.

Ed tightened his grip on Hadley's wrist, forcing the muzzle of the automatic down against Hadley's belly. His hand moved down, covered Hadley's hand. If he squeezed now, Hadley's hand would contract upon the trigger under his pressure and the gun would explode into Hadley's stomach.

From downstairs they heard the outer door open and close again. Voices came up to them from below.

Buxton groaned again and the woman hissed, "Shut up you fool! There's people in the house!"

Her long face, sitting at an angle on her neck as she looked down at him, reminded Ed of a horse. She squinted along the sights of the revolver, said speculatively, "You're an awful tough guy. Too tough to stay alive. We've got the ten thousand already. Now you've about balled up our chances of getting the second ten thousand. I wonder if my best bet wouldn't be to bump you both off right now, and then go down and say I had found out you were keeping the kid up here?"

Ed scowled, keeping his grip on Buxton's hand. The childish

voice from next door came to them again: "It's dark, and I'm hungry," followed by a burst of terrified sobbing.

Buxton stopped groaning. The woman's smile gave place to a worried frown. "If that kid yells any louder, they'll hear her downstairs. I ought to stop her."

Ed's eyes were smouldering. The sobbing inside grew louder.

Ed glared at the woman. "You've doped that poor kid, and kept her in there without food for three days! Nice people!"

He raised his left fist, brought it down hard against the side of Buxton's head. Buxton's head lolled on the floor and his grip on the automatic relaxed.

THE ADVANTAGE which Ed Race's stage training had given him over other people was that he could always coördinate the movements of all the muscles of his body—that he could do two or three things at the same time, as when he juggled revolvers while doing somersaults across the stage.

Now, his swift, perfectly-timed action would have caught the admiration of any theatre audience if he had been on a stage. For, almost as his fist struck Buxton's head, he launched his body upward, and his shoulder caught the woman's wrist, knocking it high and sending the revolver flying out of her grip.

He pushed her hard and she went sprawling backward into a corner of the room. She sat there in the corner, dazed, as Ed caught his revolver in mid-air with his left hand, transferred it to his right, then swooped down and picked up Hadley's automatic.

He was out of the room in a flash, swung the door to, and snapped the padlock on. The woman was now a prisoner in that room with Buxton. He heard her voice from behind the door shouting curses at him.

He rushed to the door of the next room, and hurled his hundred-and-ninety pounds at the door. As his weight struck it, the boards shook. The childish sobbing inside changed to a cry of terror.

Ed called out reassuringly, "It's all right, girlie, I'll get you out of there in a minute."

From down below, a heavy, angry voice shouted up, "What's going on up there? Who's up there?"

Ed didn't bother to answer. He stepped back a few paces, smashed into the door once more. It gave this time, and he went sprawling into the darkened room. He straightened, turned, and looked around.

A wee small voice said to him, "Ooh, mister—you busted the door!"

The little light that came in from the hall showed Ed a large mattress on the floor, upon which lay a kicking, squirming bundle. Wet blue eyes looked up at him out of a white, childish face topped by soft golden hair. The girl was no more than twelve years old.

"Don't let my uncle or Emma get me," she begged pitiably. "Or that bad Mr. Buxton."

Ed had gotten out a clasp knife, which he opened. He cut the cords that held the child's wrists and ankles, lifted her up in his arms. She turned her face and wiped her eyes against his coat. Then she looked up at him again and said, "My name is Alice. What's your name?"

Ed gulped. "My name is Ed," he told her.

He carried her out into the hallway, and started down the steps leading to the floor below. He heard heavy feet coming up the stairs from the ground floor, heard a harsh, angry voice saying, "We'll see what's happening up there for ourselves."

Then he heard Hadley's worried voice. "I tell you, Captain, it's only my housekeeper. She's eccentric. She lives in the attic, and I never bother her."

Ed laughed harshly, held the child closer to him. He carried the child downstairs, met Hadley, Captain Manners, and two other men in plain clothes on the first floor landing.

Manners exclaimed, "What the hell is this! You're the guy we met at the theatre!"

Ed said bitterly, "Yeah. And I have a swell story to tell you. What—*Stop him!*"

Hadley had halted midway up the stairs behind the plainclothesmen, and had now turned, and was running downstairs again. The two officers leaped after him. One of them shouted, "Hold it, you!"

Ed yelled out, "Get that guy! He's in this!"

Hadley looked back at them, his face white in the dimly-lit hallway. He snarled, "You'll never get me!"

HE SWUNG out of the door, slammed it behind him. At the same time the heavy service revolvers in the hands of the two plainclothesmen thundered in the narrow hallway, smashed through the glass and wood of the front door. From outside there came a high pitched shriek, the thud of a falling body.

The two policemen rushed outside. Ed followed Captain

Manners down into the living room, deposited the child on the settee.

In a moment one of the plainclothesmen came back, looking glum. "Hadley's dead, Cap," he reported.

Manners sighed. "All right, Stoddard. Call the coroner." He turned, looked at Ed. "Was the girl here all the time?" he asked.

Ed nodded. "They had her upstairs in the attic. The whole kidnap stunt was framed. Hadley's idea was to get Jake Landor, the boss of the Midwest, to lend him the money. When they got the first ten thousand so easy, they tried to get a second ten thousand." He grinned sourly. "When they found out that they were getting me instead of the second ten thousand, they arranged to get rid of me quick. They staged that little ruckus over at the station, where the poor pickpocket got it instead of me, and then they followed me to the theater, tried again. They had Hadley come over to put the finger on me. He sure did, too."

Captain Manners grunted. "It looks like their fingers got twisted. You sure shot straight, there in front of the theatre!"

Ed waved the compliment away. He turned to Stoddard. "Go upstairs and you'll find a surprise package waiting for you in the attic—the housekeeper, and a guy named Buxton. They were all in on the deal."

Stoddard called to his partner outside. They both went upstairs.

In the living room, Captain Manners stood looking down at Ed Race, who had seated himself beside the little girl, and was stroking her hair while she rested her head snugly against his shoulder.

Manners said, "It's a hell of a note for the poor kid. She's got no parents. Hadley was the only one in the world to take care of her. Now she's got nobody."

"Yes she has," Ed told him. He looked down at the little girl, his eyes becoming soft. "How would you like for me to adopt you, Alice?" he asked. "I'm an actor. I travel from city to city, and act in all the theaters. You could travel around with me. You'd have a swell time. Would you like it?"

She rubbed her golden hair against his shoulder and raised her eyes. "I'd love it. Are you going to be my new daddy?"

Ed glanced up at Captain Manners. "Wait'll you see her juggle guns five years from now! We'll play the Trout City Theater and I'll give you a free pass, Cap."

DEATH'S BOOKING AGENT

ED RACE stirred fretfully as the insistent clamor of the telephone, jangling against his ears, broke up his sleep. He opened his eyes. Sunlight was streaming into his eighth-floor hotel window, over the foot of the bed.

He took a minute to orient himself, lying quietly in his pajamas, while the 'phone still rang. This was the Elton Hotel, Nevada City. He'd gotten in at six in the morning, after a seven-hour flight from Chicago. Tired and cramped, he'd showered and snatched a bit of sleep before rehearsal time. The alarm clock on the dresser said nine-thirty—he could have had a good two hours more of sleep, if the telephone hadn't rung.

He swore under his breath, picked it up, growled into it. But he sat up abruptly as he recognized the voice at the other end.

"Ed, this is Nora Kirk!"

He was wide awake. "Hello, Nora, girl." His broad, powerful face softened momentarily. "Anybody else woke me up after three hours sleep, I'd massacre him. How's things? I got your dad's wire in Chicago, and made them rearrange my booking so I could play the Kirk Theater for the anniversary. Got in town just after the milkman, and didn't want to break up your beauty sleep"—he chuckled—"which is more consideration than you had for me."

Nora Kirk's voice sounded a bit strained. "It's fine of you, Ed.

Dad was sure you'd manage it. But—" She faltered a bit. "Oh, Ed—the anniversary wasn't the real reason why dad wired you. Ed, we're in trouble—terrible trouble! Can you—"

Ed lost the next words because just then someone started rapping sharply on the door of his room. He frowned, said, "Wait a minute, Nora. There's someone at the door."

He started to put the 'phone down, heard Nora crying, "Ed, don't—" Then the rapping started again, and her words were drowned out. He said, "I can't get you, Nora. Hold on while I get rid of this pest."

He put the French 'phone down on the night table, and his bare feet pounded across the floor. He turned the key, yanked the door open, growled, "Say, what—" and stopped. He was staring straight into the muzzle of a blued-steel automatic.

A cold-eyed, smiling man with flashing white teeth held the gun on him. There was another, shorter man, behind him in the corridor, also with a gun.

The white-toothed man said, "Don't be alarmed, Mr. Race. You won't be harmed if you're nice. On the other hand—"

He pushed into the room, the muzzle of the gun less than an inch from Ed Race's chest. His companion followed him in, shutting the door as he entered.

Ed backed before the white-toothed man until he was in the center of the room. Then he said, talking very loud, "I never argue with the business end of a gun, mister. The house is yours. What's this—a stick-up, or just a friendly call?"

Neither of the two callers noticed that the French 'phone was off the instrument, for Ed stood so as to conceal it from their view. The white-toothed man said, "We're not stick-ups, Mr. Race. We're just taking you along to talk to a friend of ours. As I told you before, if you behave you won't be hurt."

He motioned with the gun. "Suppose you start getting dressed."

The second man, as if everything had been pre-arranged, went across the room to the chair where Ed had flung his clothes on going to bed. He stuck his hand into the armpit holster which hung with the coat on the back of the chair, pulled out the heavy .45 Ed always carried, and handled it admiringly.

"Say!" he exclaimed to his companion. "This is some cannon, ain't it, Hone! I bet these slugs could plow through an elephant!"

The white-toothed man, addressed as Hone, continued to smile, but he said in a thin voice, "Listen, Kranz, did we come here on business or to admire hardware? Get busy!" The last he said with a snap. Kranz scowled, but did not answer. He stuck the revolver in his back pocket, carried the clothes over to the bed.

"Go ahead, big boy," he said to Ed. "Climb into them—quick!"

ED LOOKED at the clothes, then at the two men. He sat down on the bed, said in a loud voice, speaking very clearly, "So your names are Hone and Kranz? And you're just paying a little social call—with guns. You want me to get dressed and go with you—is that it?"

Hone grinned, showing his white teeth. "You seem to be pretty quick on the uptake, Mr. Race. That's about the idea. Maybe you get the idea too that we mean business. Suppose you start climbing into those clothes of yours—before we get nasty."

Ed shrugged, got up, and started to strip off his pajamas. He said, "I just wanted to get the thing straight, that's all. It always pays to understand what things are about."

As he got into his clothes, Kranz' admiring gaze wandered over his perfectly proportioned body. "Boy!" he exclaimed. "You got some muscles! How do you keep in trim?"

"Exercise," Ed told him. "I exercise every day."

Hone sat down comfortably in a chair across the room from the bed. He crossed his legs, rested the barrel of his gun on his knee, and said pleasantly to Kranz, "He's an actor. All actors keep in condition—especially guys who juggle guns, like him."

Ed's eyes narrowed. He deliberately slowed the dressing process. He wanted time to think.

Very few people knew that he juggled guns on the stage for a living. He was billed throughout the country as "The Masked Marksman." He appeared on the stage with his features concealed by a mask, and did almost incredible stunts with his heavy .45's—mates of the one Kranz had just taken from his pocket. The feats of marksmanship and juggling he performed on the stage had earned a national reputation for his act, but his identity had been pretty successfully concealed from the general public. One of the reasons why he had continued to keep his identity secret was because he dabbled in detective work on the side, carrying licenses in a dozen states to operate as a private detective.

In the pursuit of that sideline, he had made many enemies among dangerous men, and he felt it was healthier for him to keep it a secret that Ed Race, the private detective, and "The Masked Marksman" were one and the same. The fact that Hone and Kranz knew who he was gave him food for reflection.

Hone broke into his thoughts, saying pleasantly, "For a guy that moves as fast as you do on the stage, Race, you're awful slow getting dressed." He stopped dawdling the gun on his knee, raised it a trifle, and his eyes focused on a spot somewhere in the center of Ed's abdomen. "You know, we don't *have* to take you along; we could slam some lead into you right here. The party you're going to see don't *have* to talk to you. So don't give any more trouble than you have to. *Get me?*"

Ed nodded. "I get you, Hone." He hurried his dressing, wriggled into his trousers. "Only I don't get why this party should want to talk to me at all, or for that matter, why you boys should want to sling lead into me. I don't recall that there's anybody in this town with a grudge against me. As a rule, I'm a pretty peaceful citizen—" He was talking quickly, desperately, in an effort to keep the eyes of Hone and Kranz from straying toward the telephone.

Hone interrupted him, laughing heartily. "Just a peaceful citizen—ha ha! That's a laugh, Kranz, ain't it! Why, he's a holy terror!" He sobered, pointed his gun at Ed. "But I'm telling you, Race, this would be a swell time for you to cultivate that peaceful habit—it's much healthier. The party you're going to see will tell you all about it."

Ed was stuffing his shirttails into his trousers. He said nothing. Suddenly he stiffened.

Hone's eyes had settled on the end table. At first, they were casual, not grasping the significance of the French 'phone, which was lying on the table off the bracket.

Ed started to talk fast again, but it was no good. The meaning of the open telephone registered suddenly, and Hone sprang to his feet, snarling, "Who's on that 'phone?"

ED'S BODY tensed. He faced Hone, glancing at Kranz at the same time, out of the corner of his eye.

"That was the Police Department," he drawled. "They wanted to know if I'd seen two suspicious looking gunmen around here. Remember how loud I talked? That instrument was open while I mentioned your names." Ed grinned genially. "So maybe you'd better put your guns away, and start getting a little peaceful yourselves."

"Nuts!" Hone sneered. Over his shoulder he growled, "Keep him covered, Kranz," and picked up the 'phone. He said, "Hello. This Miss Kirk?"

Ed heard Nora Kirk's voice talk into the instrument, but he could not distinguish the words. Hone listened a while, then shrugged, threw a swift side glance at Ed, said into the 'phone, "Well, it's up to you, Miss Kirk. Your old man started this by sending for him. He shouldn't have sent for him in the first place. Now it's up to you to get rid of him. Here, you can do it yourself." He extended the instrument to Ed, growled, "She wants to talk to you."

Ed had his coat and vest on by this time. He took the 'phone, said, "Hello, Nora, what's all the excitement about? Why didn't you hang up and call the police when you heard what was happening here?"

Nora Kirk sounded worried, harassed. She said desperately, "Ed, you mustn't antagonize those men. Dad is in terrible trouble, and they're the only ones who can get him out of it. He shouldn't have sent for you. But now, won't you please go with them? They don't mean you any harm, and you must do whatever they say—for Dad's sake."

Ed frowned. "Sounds screwy to me, Nora, but if you say so—all right. Suppose you give me an idea what it's all about."

"I can't, Ed. I can't talk on the telephone. They'll tell you everything. Go along with them quickly now, please, and do whatever they say. I'll meet you later."

Ed hung up as Nora clicked the receiver down at her end of the line. He faced the two men, raised his eyebrows. "You boys seem to be riding high, wide and handsome. It's your show, and you're giving the cues. So what do we do next?"

Kranz uttered a sigh of relief. Hone seemed to be happier, too. Apparently they hadn't relished the job of escorting Ed Race out of the hotel and through the streets of the town at the point of their guns.

Hone said, "That's much better, Race. We'll be able to transact our business in short order as soon as you see this party we're taking you to."

Kranz started to leave, and Hone jerked his thumb toward the doorway, grinned. "You next, Race. I'll come last." He put his gun in his outside coat pocket, nodded significantly. "Remember this gat in my pocket, in case you should change your mind, or get a brainstorm."

Ed followed Kranz out along the corridor. In the elevator, Kranz stood next to him on his left, while Hone stood slightly behind. Gaining the street, they walked around the corner and entered a sedan which was parked there.

Hone sat in the rear next to Ed, while Kranz drove. They had both lapsed into a sort of sullen silence now. Hone sat slantwise at his end of the seat, his hand in the pocket where the gun was. He kept his eyes steadily on Ed, watchful for his slightest move. KRANZ WOUND skillfully in and out through traffic, driving well within the lawful speed limit. He turned into Main Street, drove through the center of town. They passed the broad gilded facade of the new glittering Kirk Theater. Men were

127

working on ladders at the side of the marquee, putting up the words which were to sparkle with electric bulbs that evening, announcing the headliners of the show. The words read:

ANNIVERSARY PERFORMANCE
THE MASKED MARKSMAN
In Person

Ed Race felt a little thrill of pleasure. He had been in vaudeville now for almost six years, but he was still able to get a kick out of seeing himself billed in the bright lights.

As they left the theater behind, Ed said: "Be careful of that revolver of mine, Kranz. Don't lose it. I'll need it for my show tonight."

Kranz did not answer, merely grunted.

In a short time they had left the town behind them, swung into a broad paved road that led northward.

Ed tried to make conversation. He asked, "How far do we go, Hone?"

Hone stirred in his seat, said tonelessly, "You'll see when we get there."

Ed shrugged. "You bozos certainly can clam up when you want to. As live entertainment, you're both a couple of complete washouts."

As they approached the crossroads, Hone stole a look ahead, then called out to Kranz, "Here it is. Turn left."

Kranz nodded, swung left at the crossing into a narrow dirt road. About a quarter of a mile farther, they swung into the driveway of what appeared to be a typical roadhouse.

Kranz halted the car under the portico, and Hone jerked his head at Ed, said gruffly, "Out!"

Ed uncrossed his long legs, opened the door and stepped out of the car.

Kranz had already alighted, and Hone followed, on Ed's other side. In that order they marched up the steps, into the deserted lobby of the roadhouse. The hat-check desk at their right in the lobby was deserted. Straight ahead, three steps down from the level of the lobby, the broad expanse of a dance floor stretched before them. At the far end was a stage, and on either side of the roped-in floor were tables and chairs which were now stacked up. There was nobody around. The place would not come to life until late at night.

They did not go onto the dance floor.

Kranz led the way up a narrow staircase at the left, extending up from the lobby. At a signal from Hone, Ed followed. Hone again brought up the rear.

On the upper floor, they stopped before a door marked "Office," and Kranz knocked three times. Without waiting for an answer, he spoke, talking through the door. "It's Kranz, Mr. Bilbo," he said. "Me and Hone. We brought him along."

A voice inside said impatiently, "All right. Bring him in."

Kranz opened the door, stood aside while Ed and Hone walked in, then, closing the door behind them, stood with his back to it.

The office was fairly large, and furnished in extremely modernistic style. At the far end, before a small square desk, sat a thin, dapper-looking man attired in a faultless morning coat.

His face was narrow at the mouth, but seemed to spread as it rose, to a broad, high forehead.

He stood up as they entered, resting long, white fingers with well-manicured nails upon the hardwood of the desk. Even in this one action the man moved lithely, gracefully, giving the effect almost of a stalking panther.

Hone started to say eagerly, "We didn't have any trouble, Mr. Bilbo. I talked to the Kirk dame and—"

Then he stopped talking very suddenly, as if he had been a radio and someone had switched him off. Bilbo hadn't said anything; had just turned and stared glassily at Hone out of his almost colorless eyes, set deep back under the wide forehead. Ed, glancing sideways at Hone, saw him lower his eyes, stare at the floor, and shuffle.

Then Bilbo said, silkily, softly, "Did I ask you, Hone?"

HONE STARTED to say something, stammeringly, but Bilbo didn't give him a chance to get it out. He turned to Ed, and said in his soft voice, "I had you brought here, Race, to talk with you. Because it would be very—er—dangerous to certain friends of yours if you went off half-cocked and spoiled our plans."

Ed stared steadily at Bilbo. "What plans?" he asked bluntly.

Bilbo's mouth smiled, though his eyes returned Ed's steady stare. He raised a white hand, waved it impatiently. "Perhaps I had better show you. It will be more convincing than telling you, and you may be more inclined to listen to reason."

He came around from behind the desk, walking effortlessly and gracefully across the room to the door. He said crisply, "Kranz and Hone—come along with us."

The corridor outside was broad, thickly carpeted, and deserted. Bilbo still led the way. The doors of all the rooms were open, and Ed could see into them. They were private dining rooms, such as a roadhouse of this type would specialize in.

Ed's eyes strayed to Bilbo's straight, narrow back. There was not a crease in his expensive coat. But there was a bulge just over the right hip pocket—a slight bulge, but quite significant. Bilbo was armed.

They proceeded to the end of the corridor, stopped before the last door on the left. That door was not open.

Bilbo dug into his pocket, extracted a set of keys. Before unlocking the door he hesitated a moment, then turned to Ed and said, "You will no doubt be surprised and shocked at what you see inside here. But be careful what you do. Above all, do not act rashly. I believe Miss Kirk told you that you were to cooperate with us."

Ed nodded. "Let's get on with this, Mr. Bilbo. You've got me all keyed up with curiosity."

Bilbo looked at Hone and Kranz, said to them coldly, "You will keep your hands on your guns while we are in the room. If Mr. Race should show a disposition to—er—become unpleasant, you know what to do."

Hone smiled pleasantly, showing his flashing white teeth. "We sure will, Mr. Bilbo. Depend on it."

Bilbo turned, inserted a key in the lock, opened the door. He entered, and Ed followed, the other two close behind him.

Bilbo took two or three steps into the room, then stepped inside for Ed to look. Ed stopped short, staring.

A tall man, about forty, sat on a chair close to the head of the bed. His wrists were handcuffed, and the links of the cuffs had been run around the bar of the bedstead, so that he was effectively imprisoned. His hair, a heavy black, graying at the temples, was disheveled, his eyes were rimmed with red. He was in evening dress, and his bow tie was askew, the collar opened at the throat. His face appeared drawn and haggard under a day's growth of bristly beard.

He looked up, seemed to have difficulty in recognizing Ed, then said listlessly, "Oh, they brought you here, Race. It's no good, though. You can't help me. I should never have sent for you. I guess I'll have to pay."

Ed wasn't listening to him, or looking at him either, for that matter. His eyes were glued to the bed. A woman lay there, on her back. She was in her thirties, and her wild, disordered hair, which was almost as red as the daring evening gown she wore, fell partly over her face, which had been beautiful. One strap of her low-cut evening gown had been torn, and the dress had fallen away from her breast, revealing a white, creamy skin.

The thing that held Ed's gaze, however, was the bone handle of the thin dagger that had pierced her throat. It protruded now at a gruesome angle. Blood had spattered the bed, and lay in dry, clotted streaks on her shoulders and chest. She was stiff, cold. She had been dead for some time.

ED'S MOUTH twisted into a thin, grim line. He whirled as Bilbo's silky voice addressed him. "Yes, Mr. Race, she is quite dead, as you see. Do you know who killed her?"

Before Ed could reply, Kirk sat up stiffly in his chair, rattling his handcuffs. "It's a lie, Race, it's a lie!" he shouted hoarsely. "I didn't kill her. I tell you, I didn't kill her." Suddenly he slumped dejectedly. "But it's all against me. I had too much to drink last night. I don't know what happened here. When I came to, I found myself handcuffed to the bed, and"—he shuddered—"there she was!" His voice dropped almost to a whisper. "Like that!"

The dapper, graceful little Bilbo smiled. "Too bad," he said, "that you drank so much last night, Mr. Kirk. You realize, of course, that your chance with a jury would be absolutely *nil.*"

Kirk closed his eyes, to shut out the sight of the corpse. "How much do you want?" he groaned.

Bilbo rubbed his hands. "Now you're talking sensibly." He turned to Ed. "What do you think, Mr. Race? Murder is a serious thing. As law abiding citizens, we should notify the police. But of course, there are ways—"

Ed had turned, was bleakly surveying the bed and its gruesome burden. He interrupted Bilbo, asked coldly, "Who is she?"

Bilbo jerked his head at the handcuffed man. "Perhaps Mr. Kirk can answer that better than I. He was out with her last night."

Kirk's face was lined, pasty. He looked sixty rather than forty. He kept his eyes studiously averted from the bed as he said, wearily, "She's Ruby Pearson. Ruby Pearson—a newcomer in vaudeville. She's been playing the Kirk Theater this week." He looked up at Ed, made a gesture of half-apology, went on pleadingly, "You can't blame me much, Race. I've been a widower for ten years now. We just went out for a little innocent fun."

"Innocent fun!" Bilbo interjected sneeringly. "It certainly ended up innocently, didn't it?"

Kirk had his head in his hands now. "I would have given everything to keep this from Nora. I'm thinking more of her now than I am of myself."

Ed said testily, "Well, let's stop the schmoozing and get down to business." He swung on Bilbo. "What do you want from Mr. Kirk?"

"Nothing much." Bilbo's eyes were sparkling eagerly now. Hone and Kranz, who were standing behind him, still with their guns in their hands, tensed as he went on. "The roadhouse business isn't so good these days. People are tight with their money. I've been wanting to get into the theatrical game. I'll swap Mr. Kirk my roadhouse for the Kirk Theater. He'll execute a deed of sale to me, and I'll send Hone down to the Registrar's Office to record it. Then he can go home and forget about this business. We'll cover it up for him."

Kirk's eyes opened wide, his hands clenched around the bedstead. "It's a million-dollar theater—and my equity in it is over three hundred thousand. And you want to give me a roadhouse for it, which isn't worth more than fifteen thousand at the outside!"

Bilbo shrugged. "Those are the terms, Mr. Kirk. Take them or leave them. Your million-dollar theater won't do you any good when you're sitting in the hot seat." He waved towards Ed. "You wanted somebody here to advise you. Well, you've got Race. I give you five minutes to decide."

Kirk had the look of a beaten man. Furtively his eyes strayed toward the cold, stiff body of Ruby Pearson on the bed. He said under his breath, "I'm licked. I'll have to do it."

Bilbo exclaimed exultantly, "Fine. I have the papers in my office. Kranz will get them. Mr. Race will sign the deed as a witness, to show that it wasn't given under duress." He said over his shoulder, "Kranz, go get the papers in the rubber band in the top drawer of my desk."

KRANZ WAS about to obey when Ed Race stopped him. "Just a minute. There's a couple of things that have to be ironed out. First, how are you going to get rid of this body?"

"Leave that to me," Bilbo told him. "There'll be no comeback."

Ed stared at him steadily. "I think Mr. Kirk is entitled to the details—*before* he signs the deed."

Bilbo said savagely, "All right. We're not getting rid of the body. It stays right here—and we let somebody else take the rap."

"The real murderer?" Ed asked him softly.

Bilbo shook his head. "No, Mr. Race, not the real murderer. Mr. Kirk's prints are on that knife handle now. We're going to take another guy, put his prints on it instead of Mr. Kirk's, and then take him out on the road, put a slug in his brain with his own gun, and leave him there. It will look just like murder and suicide."

"Very interesting," Ed murmured. "And have you got this other man picked out yet?"

"Yes, Mr. Race, we have him picked out. We also have his gun."

Ed threw a side glance at Kirk. The theater owner was slumped down in his chair, his forehead resting against the bedstead, his eyes closed. He was paying no further attention to what was going on in the room. The significance of what was being said escaped him entirely.

Ed's arms hung slack at his side as he faced Bilbo, but his body was tense, and he was teetering on the balls of his feet. "So I'm to be the fall guy, eh?"

His eyes narrowed to mere slits as he surveyed the three men. The guns of Hone and Kranz were trained upon him unwaveringly. "Very pretty. Very pretty, indeed. So that's why you were so willing to let Kirk have a friend come here. And I turned out to be the ideal friend for the purpose, huh?"

Bilbo, standing directly in front of Ed, must have correctly interpreted the look in Race's eyes. For he made a quick step backward, snapped over his shoulder to Hone and Kranz, "Take him, boys! Take him quick!"

But he was too late.

Ed moved with the quick, synchronized rhythm of muscle and body that he had developed through years of arduous work on the stage. He stepped in, his right hand flashed up, seized Bilbo by the lapels of his coat, and yanked him forward.

Bilbo uttered a frightened cry, started to kick and squirm. But Ed lifted him from the floor, held him helpless in his powerful grip. Bilbo's body now formed a shield against the guns of Hone and Kranz.

The two gunmen stood bewildered for a second with leveled guns, but afraid to shoot. And in that second, Ed took a quick leap forward, pushing Bilbo ahead of him. He crashed the squirming roadhouse proprietor square into Hone, who went stumbling backward against the wall. Almost as a continuation of the same motion, Ed swiveled and hurled Bilbo against Kranz.

Kranz sidestepped, and Bilbo's body crashed to the floor.

Kranz was snarling now, and swinging his gun around. But Ed had swooped down, seized Hone's wrist, twisted it—and snapped the automatic from his weakened grip.

Kranz lowered the muzzle of his gun, but Ed dropped flat to the floor, rolled away from Hone. Kranz' gun exploded, and a slug tore into the floor. Ed rolled to his back, looked up, saw Kranz above and behind him, and raised the automatic, squeezed the trigger. He had done this stunt often on the stage, shooting out candles while lying on his back. Kranz was a bigger target than a candle, and the steel-jacketed slug from the automatic caught him squarely between the eyes.

His gun exploded once more harmlessly into the air as he crashed backwards swiftly and struck the floor, dead.

ED, MOVING lithely, gracefully, got to his feet in time to see Bilbo dragging a small revolver from his hip pocket. Ed started to jump at him, to kick the gun out of his hand, but Hone stuck out a foot and tripped him. Ed stumbled headlong just as Bilbo shot off his revolver. The bullet clanged into the metal bedstead, ricocheted to the ceiling. Ed fell forward full length, his elbow catching Bilbo in the temple, smashing his head down hard against the floor.

Race twisted around into a sitting position, facing Hone, and said pleasantly, "All right, pal, you lose. Just stay still."

Ed stepped over to Hone, towered above him, strad-dle-legged. "Where are the keys?" he demanded.

Hone's white-toothed smile was no longer in evidence. He quavered weakly, "What keys?"

"To the handcuffs, rat."

Hone threw a glance toward Bilbo's body. "He's got them—in his pocket."

Ed backed away from him, stooped to Bilbo's pocket, dug out the ring of keys, stepped across to Kirk, inserted the key and flipped the cuffs open.

Kirk said, "Good God, Race, what'll we do now?"

Ed said grimly, "Guess what!"

He took out his handkerchief, leaned across the bed gingerly, and wiped clean the bone handle of the knife which protruded from Ruby Pearson's throat.

Kirk exclaimed in a hushed voice, "God! She was so young and full of life last night!"

Ed paid no attention to him, but turned, stamped across to Hone and seized him by the coat.

Hone demanded hoarsely, "What—what are you going to do?"

Ed didn't answer. He dragged him across to the bed, seized him from behind, and forced his right wrist over the dead woman's body. Hone struggled, but Ed twisted his left arm behind him in a punishing grip, held him there. Sweat broke out on Hone's face; his resistance ceased. Ed pushed him forward, pressed his right hand around the handle of the knife, held it there a minute, then released it.

He thrust Hone into the chair Kirk had occupied a moment ago, then snapped the handcuffs about his wrists, chaining him to the bedstead just as Kirk had been chained.

Hone stared up at him stupidly. "What—what—" he started to say.

Ed grinned down at him. "It's the same act," he told him easily. "Only the lead is played by you instead of Kirk. The way the story lines up now, you killed Ruby Pearson, and shot Kranz yourself. This is your automatic, isn't it?"

Hone had grown pale. He said, "You can't do that to me, Race. I didn't kill her. I swear I didn't kill her."

Ed told him coldly, "That's what Kirk was saying a little while ago. You boys didn't give him any break on it, did you?"

"Listen," Hone cried desperately, "don't plant this on me. I didn't kill her. Bilbo killed her himself."

Ed veiled his eyes to hide the triumph in them. "That's what I was trying to get at," he murmured. "Give me the story. Maybe if you talk enough you can beat the chair and get off with a jail sentence."

"Okay, okay," Hone said eagerly. "Ruby was Bilbo's girl. He went mad jealous when he saw Kirk bringing her up in here. He waited till they both got pie-eyed, then he came in and stuck the knife in her. That was when he got the idea of putting the screws to Kirk for the theater. Kirk was out completely and didn't know what had happened."

"You'll put that in writing?" Ed demanded.

Hone nodded. "Yes. Sure I will."

Hone had finished the statement and signed it, when Kirk called out hoarsely, "Ed, Bilbo's coming to."

Ed swung, met the dazed glance of Bilbo, who asked weakly, "What's happened?"

Ed stepped over to Kranz' body, retrieved his own heavy revolver from Kranz' back pocket. Then, straightening, he grinned down at Bilbo.

"Plenty has happened," he informed him. "The show is almost over. All the headliners have done their turn. The last act in the show will be when you get your head shaved and walk down to the hot seat."

Ed looked at his wristwatch, turned to Mr. Kirk. "See if you can find a 'phone, and call the police. We'll just about have time after that to go and give Nora the glad news, and then make the rehearsal!"

DEATH TAKES AN ENCORE

WHEN ED RACE descended from the train in Grand Central Station, after his tour of the Midwest Vaudeville Circuit, he was surprised to be met by a reception committee. It was a committee of one, and it consisted of a gentleman by the name of Dave Sayre, sergeant of detectives attached to the Homicide Bureau.

Ed didn't see the sergeant until he had turned his bag over to a porter. He started to follow the redcap, then stopped and turned as someone tapped him on the back.

"Hello, Dave," he said, "what brings *you* down here? Looking for corpses in Grand Central Station?"

Sayre ignored Ed's bantering tone. The sergeant's homely face remained grave as he took Ed by the arm. "The inspector wants to see you, Race," he said. "And it's no joke."

Ed stared at him, then asked sardonically, "What's the trouble now? I haven't gone and killed anybody, have I?"

"That's just what the inspector wants to see you about. Sorry, Race, but your first stop is headquarters."

Ed shrugged. "I don't know what it's all about, but you're the law, so I guess I better go."

He got the redcap, checked his bag, and walked out with Dave Sayre through the Park Avenue exit, got into a headquarters car which was waiting there.

The detective sergeant was singularly uncommunicative on the drive downtown. Ed Race didn't say much either. He was more or less peeved, inclined to think that Sayre was playing some sort of practical joke on him. He had had several brushes with the Homicide Bureau in the past, but all in all he was on pretty friendly terms with them, though neither Inspector Hansen nor Sergeant Sayre would admit it. They respected him highly, though he was often a thorn in their side.

Ed Race was a vaudeville juggler—a headliner. He worked with forty-five caliber revolvers, doing almost incredible feats with the heavy weapons. So expert had he become that his act was featured throughout the country, and he could have lived very comfortably on his income, if he had not had the misfortune to suffer from an insidious urge for excitement.

This urge for excitement had caused Ed Race long ago to procure for himself licenses as a private detective in about a dozen states. He had gotten himself into some pretty tight spots as a result of his interest in crime, but his supreme skill with a gun, as well as the marvelous control which he had developed over his muscles through continuous practice of his acrobatic juggling act, had always got him out, thus far, with a whole skin. He had made plenty of enemies, as well as some fast friends, and had earned the wholesome respect of men like Sergeant Sayre and his superior, Inspector Hansen. But he didn't relish the idea of being dragged down to headquarters in such summary fashion immediately upon his arrival in the city. He had a lot of other things he'd wanted to do.

DOWNTOWN, IN the big, cool gloomy building on Centre Street, Sayre led him into the inspector's private office.

Doctor Cole, one of the assistant medical examiners, was bending over Hansen's desk, talking to him in a low voice. When they entered, the doctor stopped talking and nodded to Ed, whom he knew fairly well.

Hansen looked up from the papers on his desk. His mouth was turned down at the corners, and he was frowning. He was a dapper man in his early fifties, and he wore spats and a blue handkerchief in his breast pocket. No one would have taken him for a hard-bitten inspector of police. He looked more like an insurance agent than anything else.

He dispensed with the greetings and clipped out: "Sit down, Race." He indicated a chair next to his desk, facing the window.

Ed didn't take the chair indicated. He walked around the desk, perched himself on the corner alongside the inspector's chair, and growled, "I realize it's April first, Hansen, but if this is your idea of an April Fool joke, it's all bananas to me. I overslept on the train, and didn't have a chance to get breakfast. I'm hungry, and if I don't wrap my arms around your neck and kiss you, it's because I'd rather wrap myself around some ham and eggs. So you'll have to excuse me if I don't go goofy with pleasure at the thought of being entertained by you!"

Hansen's face flushed, and he pushed himself up from the chair. He was not quite as tall as Ed, and even though Ed was sitting on the desk, he had to raise his eyes to the juggler as he shook a finger in his face. "Damn it, Race, you lay off the wisecracks and answer a few question now. Maybe you don't know it, but you're going to be booked down here. Booked for murder!"

Ed raised his eyebrows. He wasn't worried, but he was very hungry. Also very curious. He settled himself. "Someone's either nuts or else has a sprained sense of humor, Hansen. Spill it."

Hansen sat down at the desk again, snatched up a sheet of paper which had been lying in front of him. Then he glanced up, pointed a finger at Ed, demanded sharply, "You worked for Jake Landor on the Midwest Vaudeville Circuit, didn't you?"

"That's right, Inspector. I just finished a four-months' tour. My contract has eight months to go, and I was coming into New York to talk to Jake about releasing me so I could go to Hollywood to take a contract with Aetna Pictures."

Hansen consulted the sheet of paper in front of him, nodded, and said, "That's right. You finished up in Meadstown on Saturday, went into Chicago, and you took the Century Limited out of Chicago at 2:15 yesterday, arriving here at nine o'clock this morning. And of course you don't know that just twelve hours before—at nine last night—Jake Landor was murdered!"

Ed jerked to his feet from the desk. "Murdered! How? By whom?"

"That," Inspector Hansen told him slowly, "is why Sergeant Sayre brought you down here. *You* are accused of murdering Jake Landor, Race!"

Ed Race looked down at the dapper inspector in silence. Landor had been more than a casual employer to him. It was Jake Landor who had originally started Ed in vaudeville with his gun juggling act eight years ago. It was Jake Landor who had built up the act, under the title of "The Masked Marksman," until now it was headlined wherever Ed appeared.

They had been good friends. It was true that they had had many differences during the past eight years, but there had been nothing of any real consequence. It took Ed several moments to regain his composure.

He said huskily, "You—you think *I* killed Jake Landor?" Suddenly his eyes blazed. "I always thought you were a pretty good cop, Hansen. But I take it all back now. You're nothing but a cheap nitwit in spats. Jake Landor is murdered, and all you have to do is sit around here and have *me* brought in for the murder? Why, I was on the Century at the time that you yourself say he was killed!"

Hansen leaned back. "Take it easy, Race. Whether you like it or not, you're accused of killing Landor. And you're going to answer my questions and like it!"

Ed stood tense, his whole body contracted, his hands clenched, staring stormily at the other. After a little while he relaxed, but did not remove his gaze from Hansen. He said in a low, dangerous voice, "I'm not answering your questions, Hansen. If you weren't masquerading as a police inspector, I'd push your face in. As it is, I'm going out of here now and find the killer of Jake Landor myself. To hell with you and your questions!"

He swung about, headed for the door.

The sergeant's big form stopped him. "Listen, Race, you know you wouldn't get to first base that way. We're treating you OK, but if you want to get roughed up, we can do it. Now, go back and behave yourself." After all, it would be easy enough to show them that he had nothing to do with Landor's death—but that he'd have plenty to do with bringing the killers in. White-lipped, he nodded, went back.

Hansen spoke quickly: "You wrote a letter to Jake Landor Saturday night from Chicago, didn't you? And you sent it to him air mail, special delivery, didn't you?"

Ed's eyes were puzzled. "Sure I did. I wanted to be sure Jake would stay in New York so I could see him this morning. What of it?"

Hansen did not take his eyes from Ed, but he jerked his head in the direction of Doctor Cole, said curtly to the medical man, "Tell him about it, Doc."

DOCTOR COLE stroked his thin, smooth-shaven face. "Landor died," he explained, "as a result of inhaling the fumes of hydrocyanic acid. The autopsy shows conclusively that this was the cause of death."

Ed was still puzzled. He glanced at Dave Sayre, who was still standing at the door, then back at the inspector. "I still don't see what that has to do with my writing a letter to Jake." He glared at Hansen. "Maybe you'll stop being mysterious and give me the lowdown."

For answer, Hansen opened the drawer of his desk, withdrew a manila folder from which he extracted an envelope with an airmail stamp. He held it gingerly between thumb and forefinger and asked, "This the letter you wrote, Race?"

Ed recognized his handwriting and nodded.

Hansen handed it across the desk to him and said very quietly, "Take a whiff of that."

Ed took the letter, asked, "Whiff? What do you mean?"

"Go on," Hansen prompted, "do as I say."

Ed raised the envelope to his nostrils and immediately got a faint odor of bitter almonds. He frowned, his thumb rubbing over what looked like the traces of some paraffin, still adhering to the inside of the envelope. He looked up at the doctor. "That's—hydrocyanic acid, isn't it?"

Cole nodded somberly. "Just the traces left. But when Landor slid the letter opener under the envelope flap, that punctured the little paraffin sac which you—ah—the criminal—had placed there for that purpose. Before he knew it, Landor had taken just one breath of that stuff. It was enough—more than enough."

Ed started. "My God, Doctor! That—that's fantastic! It's my letter, all right, but I certainly didn't fix any paraffin sac filled with hydrocyanic in the thing. It—it's—" He shook his head.

Hansen got up from behind the desk, thrust his jaw forward. "Now do you see why you were brought down here, Race?"

Ed's face was white, strained. "I get it," he said, low-voiced. "Sorry, Hansen, I couldn't see how you figured me for killing Jake while I was on the Century. I thought you were being bull-headed or smart, or something."

Hansen didn't answer him, but motioned to Dave Sayre. "Send in the two witnesses, Dave."

The sergeant left the room, returned in a few minutes with two men. Ed knew both of them.

One was Bert Dorsey, Jake Landor's secretary. The other was Thayer Zachary, the head of Middle States Vaudeville Enterprises, Inc., the leading rivals of the Midwest Vaudeville Circuit.

Thayer Zachary was a man in his middle fifties, tall, powerfully built, with a commanding appearance. He had his finger in a number of pies, was interested in motion pictures as well as in vaudeville.

He nodded curtly to Ed, said to Inspector Hansen, "You will oblige me by getting through with this as quickly as possible, Inspector. I am a busy man."

"That's all right, Mr. Zachary," Hansen told him. "I realize you are a busy man, but this is murder. It takes precedence over business."

Bert Dorsey, a small, mouse-like man of thirty-eight or forty, turned watery blue eyes upon Ed Race in reproachful fashion.

His mouth trembled as he said, "Y—you had no business killing poor Mr. Landor—after all he'd done for you, Race. Damn you, you've killed my employer, and now I've got no job!"

Ed was silent, but Hansen snorted. "Lay off that stuff, Dorsey. You ought to be damn glad you didn't open the letter yourself." He seated himself behind the desk, pointed a finger at the secretary. "Now tell us what happened when that letter came."

Dorsey sniffled, proceeded in a hesitant voice. "I was home with Mr. Landor when it came. I answered the doorbell and signed for the letter. Ordinarily I would have opened it, if it came in the regular mail, but Mr. Landor was in the sitting room, so I brought it right in to him. I had been working on some accounts at the desk in the corner. I handed him the letter and started back for the desk. Suddenly I heard a gasp, and I turned around to see Mr. Landor jerking in his chair with awful sort of convulsions. He had dropped the letter to the floor."

Dorsey shuddered, closed his eyes and gulped.

"Go on," Hansen urged him in a kindly voice. "What happened then?"

"I dashed up to him to see if there was something I could do, to see what was the matter. Mr. Landor's face was getting bluish. Suddenly he slipped from the chair to the floor, as if he was paralyzed. He seemed to be strangling. I rushed for the 'phone, but before I got the connection he was dead!"

Dorsey raised his hand, pointed a shaking finger at Ed. "He did it, he did it!" he almost shrieked. "He did it because Mr. Landor wouldn't release him to act in the movies!" Dorsey sank into a chair, covered his face with his hands.

ED RACE had listened tensely to the account. He saw that Thayer Zachary's eyes were upon him, and he said calmly, "What do you think, Mr. Zachary—do you think I killed Jake Landor?"

Zachary regarded him coldly. "I am quite sure you did, Race."

Ed took a step in Zachary's direction, his face a dull red.

Dave Sayre stepped between them. "Take it easy, Race," he soothed. "Wait'll you hear what Mr. Zachary has to say."

Zachary went on impassively, addressing himself to Inspector Hansen. "As I told you before, Inspector, I had had lunch with Landor earlier in the day. He told me he was worried about Race; said that he had talked to him on long distance twice during the week, and that Race had been angry with him for refusing to release him from the contract. He said Race claimed he could make fifteen thousand dollars a week for ten weeks in Hollywood and that Landor was keeping him from making the money for spite. He said Race had become quite violent over the 'phone."

Hansen bent his shaggy brows upon Ed. "Do you deny that?"

Ed had difficulty controlling himself. "I did talk to Jake twice, but we didn't have any such argument. Jake merely asked me to wait until I got back to New York to talk about it, because things were pretty well up in the air for him, personally. He said there was a possibility that he might have to sell out his holdings in the Midwest Vaudeville Circuit, and that I better wait a week until he knew where he stood. I readily agreed. There were no arguments or threats between us."

"That's what *you* say," Hansen sneered. "On the face of the evidence that is presented here, I think we'll have to hold you for the D.A." He turned to the two witnesses. "You may go now, Mr. Zachary and Mr. Dorsey. But please be ready to come down to the District Attorney's office to tell your story later in the afternoon. The D.A. will probably take you right before the Grand Jury and get an indictment."

Zachary bowed, cast a cold glance at Ed, and left the room, followed by Dorsey, who still seemed to be suffering from nervous shock.

Ed was restraining himself with difficulty. He was seeing red for the first time in his life. He had been in tight jams before, but never had he been faced with such damning evidence. When the door had closed behind the two witnesses, he swung about, blurted at Hansen: "What sort of sap do you take me for? If I had wanted to kill Jake, would I do it that way—wouldn't I know that my letter would be found with that stuff in it?"

Hansen shook his head sourly. "Lots of guys do crazy things. The evidence is against you."

"You mean," Ed demanded hotly, "that you're going to hold me—have me indicted for murder?"

"That's just what I mean, Race."

Hansen motioned to the detective sergeant. "Take away his artillery, Dave. Then take him downstairs and have him booked and fingerprinted. If he wants a lawyer, he can get one." He looked up at Ed. "I'm sorry as hell about this, Race. I used to think a good deal of you. And I hope to hell you can clear yourself of this charge. Believe me, I'm sincere about that."

Dave Sayre stepped up to Ed, looking apologetic, and reached a hand toward Ed's shoulder holster.

Ed's face was grim, determined. He was not going to be locked up. He sidestepped swiftly, putting the sergeant between himself and Hansen. At the same moment his left hand came up, palm outward, and *smacked* square into Dave Sayre's face.

Ed murmured, "Sorry, Dave, I got to do this."

Ed's arm straightened behind the opened palm, sending Sayre toppling into Hansen's desk. The sergeant fell backward over the glass top, his hands spread-eagled on either side of him in a frantic endeavor to regain his balance. But he couldn't stop, smashing into Hansen's gun hand before the inspector could spring backwards for a clear shot at Ed.

Ed Race streaked for the door, yanked it open. The last thing he saw as he closed the door behind him was the gaping, open mouth of Doctor Cole, who stared at him in astonishment.

Ed hurried toward the rear of the hall, slipped out through a side exit just as he heard Hansen's stentorian bellow behind him.

A uniformed policeman who had been strolling down the hall swung about, tugging for his revolver. But Ed was already outside. He sped around the corner, hailed a cab, and swung himself into it.

"Uptown," he ordered curtly. "And don't wait."

THE DRIVER turned startled eyes as he heard shouts from around the corner, but Ed got out his heavy forty-five caliber revolver, pressed it into the driver's back. "Did you hear what I said?" he asked softly.

The driver was too scared to talk. He merely faced forward, automatically threw the car into gear, and shot ahead just as

Hansen's bulky form appeared around the corner behind them, followed by Dave Sayre and half a dozen bluecoats.

"Turn right at the next corner," Ed commanded.

The cabby obeyed. Then, at Ed's instructions, he made a left turn at the next corner, headed northward again.

Ed knew that the alarm would be out for him in a matter of moments. As they drove uptown he kept a watchful eye out for radio cars, but they encountered none. They passed a couple of traffic officers, but these had not yet been apprised that there was a chase on.

At Twenty-third Street, Ed got out of the cab, gave the driver a ten-dollar bill. He now had his revolver in his overcoat pocket. "Get going!" he ordered.

The cabby took the ten-dollar bill half reluctantly and ground off. Ed watched him till he had rounded the corner, then hurried back to a cab stand, got another cab and drove across town to Eighth Avenue. Here he changed cabs once more, drove uptown to the Forties, and got out. He walked east on a side street till he came to a little store in the basement of a private house. The built-in window was littered with junk and knickknacks. The only lettering on the window was the name *Gibson's*.

Ma Gibson, who ran this little junk store, came running from the rear with a glad cry when she saw who it was. She was a buxom woman, and she had pinpoint eyes. Her face, however, despite the small eyes, reflected boundless good nature.

Ed had done her many a favor in the past, had once saved her only daughter from a miserable fate at the hands of a dope ring. He knew he could depend upon her to the limit—and no questions asked.

"Look, Ma," he said urgently, without any preliminary greetings, "I got to hide out here till tonight. How's that little secret room in the cellar where you used to cache swag—still working?"

Ma Gibson, as he had expected, asked no questions. She turned and led the way to the rear, then down a flight of steps to the cellar.

Ma Gibson's face was creased with worry. She exclaimed solicitously, "Is it bad, Ed? Who's after you?"

"The cops. They think I killed Jake Landor."

"Well, of all the damn fools! Don't they know that you and Jake were the best of friends?"

Ed shrugged. "I've got to prove I didn't kill him. I'll need to get around a little. Think you can drop over to Jennings' Theatrical Agency and pick me up some makeup stuff so I can change my face a little—just enough to fool them in the dark? And you might bring along whatever you've got in the ice-box. I'm still starving!"

Ma Gibson nodded vigorously. "Of course, I will, Ed. And if you want me to go down to headquarters and give that spalpeen of an Inspector Hansen a piece of my mind, I'll gladly do it!"

"Don't bother, Ma." Ed patted her shoulder. "I'll attend to that part of it. Don't worry about me. Just get me the stuff, and I'll manage."

After she had closed the door, Ed sat in his little cubby-hole and concentrated on the problem. He took out the two heavy forty-five caliber revolvers that he carried in the twin holsters under each armpit. Reverently he laid them on the table, took out his handkerchief and polished them.

THESE WERE two of the half-dozen guns that he used in his phenomenal juggling act, which had carried the country by storm. Ed could do things with those heavy revolvers that were almost incredible. When he went through the routine of his number on the stage, the perfect coördination of his mind, his eye and the muscles of his body produced effects of marksmanship that were well-nigh superhuman.

Eight years of rigid training as a vaudeville juggler and marksman served to keep his superb body continuously in condition. And he gave his guns as much attention as he gave to himself. Every day they were cleaned, and the cartridges were examined for defects.

Now, as Ed unloaded them, blew microscopic specks out of the chamber and then reloaded them, he thought bitterly of Jake Landor, lying dead in the police morgue with the scent of bitter almonds about his body. It was Jake Landor who had devised the slogan which had carried Ed to fame across the country: "The Masked Marksman—The Man Who Can Make Guns Talk."

Ed finished reloading the guns, making sure that the chamber under the hammer in each was empty. This was for his own protection, as the closely filed hair-trigger needed little coaxing to go off.

Ma Gibson was away for almost an hour and a half. Ed was beginning to be worried about her when he heard a scraping sound on the other side of the wall, and the hidden door began to swing open.

But Ed was taken entirely by surprise at sight of the figure who faced him. Thayer Zachary stood in the doorway, his hand gripping an automatic which was trained squarely on Ed's stomach.

Zachary had the darkness of the cellar behind him, and Ed's room was lighted. There was no chance for Ed to draw in the face of that murderous automatic. Zachary's face was set, his eyes fixed with a deadly purpose.

He said, "Stand still, Race." Then he called out over his shoulder, "Bring her in."

He sidestepped into the room, left the doorway open, and in a moment Dorsey appeared with Ma Gibson. He held her hands twisted behind her back in a cruel, merciless grip.

Dorsey was no longer the shy, frightened, mouse-like man that he had been in Inspector Hansen's office. His eyes were bloodshot, his thin lips were drawn back from discolored teeth. He retained his grip on Ma Gibson's arms, and she winced as he twisted them upward. There was a flaming red mark on her arm above the elbow, which was rapidly blistering.

Her fat, usually good-natured face was twisted in agony as she blurted out, "I couldn't help it, Ed. They knew you were here. They dragged me into the back of the store and gagged me, and then they heated an iron and put it to my arm. I couldn't stand it. I had to tell them about this room. I—"

Her rapid, almost hysterical flow of words was abruptly checked by Dorsey, who slammed her body against the wall so that the breath was knocked out of her.

"Shut up, you!" he growled.

Ed's eyes flamed. He took a half step forward, but stopped as Zachary thrust his automatic out at him. Zachary was cold, fully in possession of himself, and, Ed realized, was the more dangerous of the two.

Zachary said softly, "Get back up against the wall, Race, and lift your hands up over your head."

Ed stalled for time. He said, "So you two boys collaborated on the scenario, eh? Which one of you killed Jake Landor?"

Zachary smiled thinly. "It doesn't matter, Race. To all intents and purposes, you are the one who killed Landor."

"I see it now," Ed said bitterly. "You wanted to buy out Jake Landor; you had to have his circuit, or go on the rocks yourself. So you bribed this little rat here"—indicating Dorsey—"and he got the hydrocyanic acid ready. Then when my letter came, he gave Jake a few whirls of the acid, and planted a couple of drops in my envelope with the paraffin. With you to back him up with your story about having had lunch with Jake earlier in the day, he was able to get away with it, and pin the rap on me. And you figured you'd be able to buy up the circuit at a bargain from the executors."

He stopped, grinned sourly as he saw in Zachary's eyes that he had hit the mark with every one of his deductions.

Dorsey, who still retained his cruel grip on Ma Gibson, spat out viciously, "Get through with this, Mr. Zachary. What's the difference what he knows? Let's finish this up and beat it!"

Ma Gibson uttered an involuntary gasp of pain as he gave her arms an extra twist to emphasize his words.

Ed's fist clenched. "You little rat!" he rapped out. "I'm going to kill you for that!"

DORSEY BURST out laughing. "You ain't going to kill anybody after today." Dorsey was not the type who would generally be expected to act in a vicious or murderous manner. But Ed could see that he was merely trying to give himself courage. He was on the verge of hysteria with the knowledge that he had actually killed his employer, Jake Landor, and was trying to buck himself up. It was amateur killers like these that were dangerous, for there was no accounting for what they might do in the heat of the moment.

Zachary, however, was the man to be reckoned with right at this time. Ed read death in the big theater man's eyes.

Zachary said softly, "That is right, Race. After today you will no longer be interested in what happens to anybody."

He stepped closer, snapped out, "Raise your hands up higher—all the way up!"

The muzzle of the automatic was close to Ed's chest. He obeyed, his eyes locking with Zachary's as he said coldly, "You're not crazy enough to think you can get away with this, are you? You were smart enough to frame somebody else for Jake's death. Whom are you going to frame for mine?"

Zachary smiled with his lips, but his eyes had a sort of cold, deadly, fish-like stare. He took a handkerchief out of his pocket, and still holding the gun on Ed, he awkwardly wrapped the handkerchief around his left hand, then reached in and jerked out one of Ed's heavy forty-fives from its shoulder holster. He was now holding the revolver with the handkerchief wrapped around the butt so as not to leave any fingerprints. Then he stepped back four paces to the door.

Ed said, "Look out for that, it's got a hair-trigger."

Zachary, still keeping his eyes on Ed, felt gingerly for the trigger of the big revolver. He called out, "All right, Dorsey, stand away from the woman. Come over here."

Dorsey let go of Ma Gibson's arms, came and stood beside Zachary. Zachary swung the big revolver in his left hand to cover both Ed and Ma Gibson, and handed the automatic over to Dorsey.

Ma Gibson had slumped back against the wall, her arms hanging limply. Her face was white from the torture.

Ed was watching Zachary closely. Suddenly he said tensely, "Listen Zachary, I can guess what you're going to do. Don't do it. Ma Gibson never harmed you. You don't have to rub her out. Let her promise to keep mum on this, and I'll give you my word to take the rap for Jake's murder."

Zachary shook his head. "I don't believe in taking any chances, Race. When people are dead, that's the only time I'm sure they can't talk."

Dorsey, whose hand holding the automatic was shaking a bit, inquired nervously, "What you going to do, Mr. Zachary?" His voice was high-pitched, at the verge of breaking.

"I'm going to kill the woman with Race's gun," Zachary told him. "Then I'll kill Race. His fingerprints will be the ones on the gun. We'll come rushing down here and find them both dead. The story will be that Ma Gibson knew he killed Jake Landor, and in a fit of rage he shot her and then shot himself. It'll go over fine. We can say that we came here because we knew that Race was in the habit of seeing Ma Gibson when he was in town. We just walked in at the tail end of the shooting."

Dorsey drew in a deep breath that sounded like a wheeze. "God, can we get away with it?"

Ed broke in hurriedly, "Of course you can't, Dorsey." He was playing on the secretary's apparent weakness and fear. "Landor is dead—you can't take that back. But you don't have to get in any deeper. You can turn state's evidence on Zachary and cop yourself a plea. How about it, Dorsey? Quick, turn that automatic on him!"

Zachary snarled, "Damn you, Race!" and backed up another step so that he now stood in the doorway, commanding Dorsey with the automatic as well as Ma Gibson and Ed.

Dorsey turned half-toward him. "Don't worry, Mr. Zachary, I'm not listening to him. I'd get twenty years in jail on a plea anyway. I'd rather take a chance with you."

"Okay," said Zachary softly. "Here goes!"

HE SWUNG the gun toward Ma Gibson, steadied it, and his finger depressed the trigger.

There was only an empty click.

Ma Gibson, who had stood silent against the wall ever since Dorsey had released her, uttered a slight gasp. Her body had been involuntarily pressing backward against the wall, shrinking from the slug that she had expected to slam into her.

At the sound of the empty click under the hammer, Zachary's face went a dead white. His eyes sought Ed, and he uttered a startled gasp of dismay. For in the split second that it had taken him to press the trigger, Ed's hand had flashed in and out from the right-hand armpit holster in a motion that was a marvelous exhibition of perfect timing. He clicked the hammer on the empty chamber, then fired as the muzzle of the revolver came level with Zachary's chest.

Zachary's body went hurtling out into the darkness of the cellar, accompanied by a choked cry of pain.

Dorsey fired his automatic with a wavering, trembling hand, and the shot went wild. But Ed's next shot caught Dorsey in the right shoulder, spun him around and crashed him against the wall. The automatic slipped from his nerveless fingers.

Ed holstered his revolver, ran over to Ma Gibson, and caught her as she was slumping to the floor. He shook her hard.

"Hold on, Ma. Don't faint, whatever you do. It's all over."

Ma Gibson didn't faint. She was made of pretty sturdy stuff. She smiled wanly, said, "I'm all right, Ed. Is Zachary dead?"

"Where I hit him," Ed told her grimly, "he ought to be good and dead by now."

Dorsey's pain-racked voice came to them from the floor. "Get me a doctor," he wailed. "I'm dying."

Ed stepped over to him, stood above him spraddle-legged. His eyes were wintry, unsympathetic. Dorsey wasn't dying. The slug had caught him high in the right shoulder, had possibly smashed the bone, but the wound was not fatal. The secretary, however, did not know this. That heavy forty-five caliber slug would make anyone that it hit think the end of the world had come.

Ed did not disabuse Dorsey of his fear. He said, "What do

you want a doctor for? You might as well kick off now, as wait to be burned."

Dorsey's shoulder was bleeding profusely; crimson stained his coat and dripped to the floor. His eyes were closed in agony, and there was sweat on his hands, his face and his neck. His collar was wilted, splashed with red.

He gasped, "I don't want—to die. Get me a doctor—save me—I'll confess. I—killed Landor. Zachary—made me do it. He knew—I had served a term for—forgery, fifteen years—ago."

Dorsey's voice died away to a whisper with the last word, his eyes remained closed, and his body collapsed on the floor.

Ed's mouth was a tight, bitter line. He flung over his shoulder to Ma Gibson, "Now what'll we do? When he comes to, he'll deny it, of course."

Ma Gibson got to her feet, walked over to him unsteadily. "Never mind, Ed, boy, the police will get a confession out of him somehow. They ought to be here. Those shots—?"

She stopped suddenly, and Ed jerked his eyes to the doorway at the faint sound of movement in the cellar beyond.

The figure of Detective Sergeant Dave Sayre appeared in the doorway, stepping over the inert body of Zachary. He held a service revolver in his hand, but it was not leveled at Ed.

He seemed to be quite happy as he said, "Don't worry about the confession, Race. I heard him just before he keeled over. Funny," he went on, stepping into the little room and holstering his gun, "I had a hunch you'd be at Ma Gibson's—only I could never have found this room by myself." He looked at Ed, and there was a strange warmth in his eyes. "You know," he said huskily, "I was pretty sure you hadn't killed Landor. I knew you weren't that kind of guy. The inspector will be glad to hear it too."

Ed grunted. He holstered his revolver, went to the body of Zachary and retrieved the other one.

Ma Gibson was sitting in the chair near the table, sobbing quietly into a small handkerchief.

Sergeant Sayre asked Ed, "What happened here? Where did these boys get the nerve to try gunplay with you?"

"Zachary had the drop on me," Ed explained. "The thing that ruined him was that he didn't know that you always keep the first chamber of the barrel empty under the hammer of a hair-trigger revolver! I thought that stunt might save someone's life someday—and it sure did!"

MURDER IN THE SPOTLIGHT

WHEN ED RACE returned to the Longmont Hotel after taking his usual morning constitutional, the clerk at the desk handed him his key, a telephone message, and a white envelope on which his name was neatly typed. The telephone message said that Mr. Partages, the owner of the Clyde Theater, would call on Ed in person in a half hour.

"Mr. Partages just called a few minutes ago, sir," the clerk explained. "I told him you always came back from your walk at about ten o'clock, and he said to be sure you waited for him—that it's important."

Ed thanked the clerk. In the elevator, on the way up to his room he slit the white envelope—and whistled softly. In it, as he found by removing them, were five one thousand dollar bills.

The elevator operator turned at the whistle, saw the money, and grinned broadly.

"Looks like you're in the dough, Mr. Race."

Ed grunted. "This is as much of a surprise to me as it is to you, Al."

While speaking, he pulled out of the envelope a small slip of paper, upon which a message had been carefully typed. The message read:

"It's better to be a live vaudeville juggler than a stiff corpse.

Take a tip from us and don't accept the job Partages is going to offer you in the Clyde Theater. The enclosed chicken feed should compensate you for not taking the job. Be smart. If you should take Partages' job, you won't have a chance to enjoy the five grand."

Ed stuffed the note in his pocket together with the bills, stepped into the corridor and walked toward his room. A surge of pleasurable excitement overtook him. For two weeks now, ever since the death of Jake Landor, the boss of the Midwest Vaudeville Circuit, he had had nothing to do but mark time until the new owners of the Circuit could arrange his booking.

He was a professional juggler, but not one of the common garden variety. He juggled neither apples nor bright red balls. His playthings on the stage were six heavy, hair-trigger .45 caliber revolvers similar to the two which he carried in his armpit holsters at this moment.

In addition to juggling the guns, he accomplished almost incredible feats of marksmanship with them. His performance was a beautiful, rhythmic symphony embodying supreme coördination of muscle, mind and eye. He was billed throughout the country as THE MASKED MARKSMAN—and wherever he appeared he never failed to pack the house.

Any other man might have been completely satisfied with such a unique position in the vaudeville world. But not Ed Race. He had long ago discovered that just as other men needed food and drink to sustain life, he himself required thrills, excitement and danger. So he had turned to the investigation of crime as a hobby. Now he had licenses to operate as a private detective in a dozen states—had he ever felt like retiring from the stage he could, he knew, have made a very comfortable living from his hobby.

Now, though it was not quite clear what this was all about, he felt confident things were going to start happening. Nobody puts five thousand dollars in an envelope without meaning business.

THE NOTE had put him on his guard: when he stepped into his room, his right hand was close to his left shoulder holster. He closed the door behind him, and his eyes swept the room with a quick, searching glance.

Nobody was in it. But he noted one thing. The little black bag on his dresser was not in quite the same position as when he had left an hour ago. He opened it, studied the four heavy revolvers inside, swathed in chamois. These, with the two he carried, constituted the important props of his juggling act. All six weapons received the loving care the owner of a racing stable would have bestowed upon a favorite thoroughbred.

Ed unwrapped one of the revolvers, broke it, and removed the cartridges from the chamber. His eyes narrowed as he saw that each shell had been tampered with—filed down, and the powder removed. They were no more than blank cartridges.

Stormy-eyed, he proceeded to reload the guns from a supply of cartridges in his trunk. He had just finished with the last when he heard a scraping noise from the bathroom, the door of which was closed. Gripping more tightly the revolver in his hand, he sprang across the room, yanked open the bathroom

166

door, twisting to one side as he did so, and leveled the gun at his hip.

But he didn't shoot.

Slowly his mouth twisted into a wry smile, and he said, "For the love of Pete, Halloran. I never thought you'd let anybody do that to you!"

Halloran, the house detective, was in the bathtub. But he had all his clothes on, and his hands were tied behind his back.

167

Nor did he answer, because one of his socks had been stuffed in his mouth, and tied in place with a handkerchief. He had been trying to maneuver himself over the side of the tub.

Ed put his gun away, and entered the room. Standing beside the tub, he burst out laughing. "Halloran," he managed to gasp out, "this is classic. I wish I had a camera!"

The house detective gurgled behind his gag, and his eyes glared expressively as Ed, still laughing, stooped and helped him out of the tub, then untied his wrists and the gag.

"So somebody gave you a sock in the mouth, huh! I bet it tastes bitter."

Halloran rubbed his wrists, glowered, then sat down and started to put on his sock and shoe.

"Maybe it's funny to you, Race," he growled, "but if I ever see the palooka that done this to me, I'll twist him so he'll be able to put his whole foot in his mouth!"

Ed asked innocently, "You mean to tell me that it took just one palooka to put you in that bathtub? You surprise me, Halloran."

The house detective finished lacing his shoe, and stood up. "He had me covered the minute I came in," he explained. "He was holding one of your guns in his hand. What could I do?"

Ed grew suddenly serious. "Tell me about it, Halloran."

"Well, I just happened to be up here on the fifth floor, and I turned the corridor and seen this bird going into your room. All I got a glimpse of was his back, and I didn't think anything suspicious about it, just figured he was calling on you. Then when

I got down stairs, I saw your key in the box, so I knew you hadn't come back yet. Get me?"

"That was very clever, Halloran," Ed told him. "You have the makings of a real detective."

HALLORAN DIDN'T spot the sarcasm. He went on pridefully. "So up I came again, and burst in here. And there was this bird, standing right by the dresser, holding onto your gun, and it just happened to be pointing straight at me! This guy was tall and skinny, with dark hair and mean eyes. And he says to me, 'Just come inside, dick, and close the door behind you, quiet.' So that's what I done. And the monkey tied me up and flung me in the bathtub!"

Ed said sympathetically, "It's a hell of a note, Halloran, when people go around attacking peaceful, defenseless house detectives. Suppose you scram now, and if you see the mean bird that tied you up, be sure to call a cop."

He propelled the detective toward the door.

Halloran looked at him dazedly. "Ain't you going to report this? That bird was going through your room!"

"If you don't mind, I'd rather not report it. As long as it is over, let's forget about it. The only thing hurt was your pride. And at that you ought to be thankful this chap didn't turn on the water when he put you in the tub. Imagine how it would have felt to get a bath!"

With the door closed behind Halloran, Ed thoughtfully took the note from his pocket, together with the five one thousand dollar bills. As he started to read the note again, the telephone rang. The clerk downstairs informed him that Mr. Leon Partages and two other gentlemen were at the desk.

Ed said, "Send them up," and put both note and money back in his pocket. Also he replaced the four revolvers in the small black bag on the dresser, and closed it. Moments later there was a knock, and he opened the door to admit the visitors. Leon Partages, with whom he shook hands, was short and fat, but there was a stubborn set to his chin which accounted for the tremendous success he had made in the theater business.

In a short, clipped manner the theater man said: "Hello, Race. Hello, hello. I want you to meet Mr. Westerman, my general manager, and Charlie Barrett my lawyer. Close that door, and let's get down to business."

Ed nodded to the others. Barrett he knew by sight. He closed the door, found chairs for the three men and sat, himself, on the bed.

Westerman perched on the edge of his chair, took out and adjusted a pair of shell rimmed glasses, and produced an envelope, which he handed over to Partages. "There you are, sir. This is what you wanted to show Mr. Race."

Charlie Barrett, who was entirely bald and looked like a politician, leaned back in his chair, crossed his legs and lit an expensive cigar. He seemed entirely at ease.

Partages took the envelope, hesitated, cleared his throat, then said: "Look, Ed, before I show you this, I got a proposition to make. I want you to put on your juggling act for the opening number at the Clyde Theater this afternoon. Your regular salary with the Midwest Vaudeville Circuit has been five hundred dollars a week; I'll give you a thousand a week."

"What's the catch?" Ed asked.

Partages leaned forward eagerly. "You're right. There *is* a catch. Here, take a look at this."

HE EXTRACTED a sheet of paper from the envelope Westerman had given him, and handed it over. It was a neatly typed message, addressed to Leon Partages. It read:

> The Clyde Theater represents an investment of a lot of money. You would lose plenty if you had to close up. If you are willing to pay ten percent of your proceeds each week, we will permit you to continue to operate. Otherwise, the first actor who appears upon the stage at each performance will be *killed*. If you are willing to pay this percentage, you may insert an ad in the Business Opportunity column of the Times. Let it read, "I will take a ten per cent partner in my vaudeville enterprises." If you insert the ad, you will receive instructions as to how to make your payments. If the insertion does not appear by Saturday, the first performer who appears in the Monday's matinee performance will die.

There was no signature.

Ed Race handed the letter back to Partages. He said thoughtfully, "This is Tuesday. I take it you didn't insert the ad?"

Partages shook his head violently. Westerman spread his hands out in a gesture of appeal. "How could we accept, Mr. Race. There would spread the system to every theater in the city if they succeeded with us."

171

Charlie Barrett, the lawyer, said nothing. He tilted his head, blew smoke rings at the ceiling.

"All right." Ed stirred impatiently. "You didn't insert the ad. So what happened yesterday?"

Partages stood up suddenly, began pacing up and down the room. "They kept their threat! You know Stackney and Vines—the acrobatic team?"

Ed nodded.

"Well, Stackney was the first to appear on the stage at yesterday's show. Their number opened the bill." He stopped in front of Ed, shook a pudgy forefinger in his face. "*Stackney was shot through the heart by somebody in the audience with a silenced rifle!*"

Westerman added: "We kept it a secret. The police didn't give out any information to the reporters. The audience didn't know Stackney had been shot. They just thought he fainted."

"I get it," Ed said. "Now you want me to go on instead of Stackney this afternoon, and be number two. Is that it?"

"Look, Ed," Partages urged appealingly, "you're the logical man to do it. You're lightning with those guns of yours, and you always go on with the whole house lighted up. There'll be plain-clothes men sitting in the aisle seats in every single row. Nobody with a large package will be admitted. There'll be danger, yes—but I know you, and I know damn well you'll do it!"

Ed sighed. "I guess you're right, Partages. I'll do it."

Partages wheezed a deep breath of relief. "I was sure you would." He smacked his right fist into his left palm. "Now I can fight these dirty murdering leeches. Look, Ed, I brought Charlie Barrett along to draw an agreement. I'm going to pay you a thousand a week. But if anything should happen to you, this agreement is going to provide to take care of any dependents you may have, for the rest of their lives. Leon Partages knows how to take care of people who do him a good turn!"

Charlie Barrett took the cigar out of his mouth, bounced to his feet, and said, "Yes, Mr. Race, it's a most liberal agreement. I had my secretary draw a rough draft. Here it is." He took a document from his vest pocket. "Suppose you look it over, and if it meets with your approval, I'll have it typed formally. You—"

A knock sounded at the door.

BARRETT STOPPED talking. Westerman inched even further forward on his chair. Partages said in a low whisper, "Who's that?"

Ed shrugged. "The best way to find out is to ask." He raised his voice. "Yes?"

"It's me—Halloran. Lemme in, quick. I got to see you important!"

Ed motioned to Barrett, who was nearest the door. "It's the house detective. He had a tussle with someone here in my room a little while ago. Better let him in before he rouses the whole hotel."

Barrett went to the door, slipped the catch. Halloran came stumbling in propelled by someone from behind. His hands were in the air, and his face was red with rage.

The man who had pushed him in stepped in also, kicked the door shut with his heel, and stood with his back against it. He was holding a Thompson sub machine gun in the crook of his elbow and the nasty little snout of it moved in a slow half circle, covering everybody in the room.

Halloran said sheepishly, "This is the same guy who tied me up in the bathroom. He was hiding out in five-nineteen, and he got the drop on me again. He made me knock on your door and say what I did say."

The man who held the machine gun was very tall, and wore a felt hat that sat low on his thin, long head. His eyes were small, set close together, and had a nasty glint. He was standing slightly behind Halloran, protected by the house detective's body.

Ed's hand was half raised to his shoulder holster, but there was no use pulling a revolver in the face of that machine gun, especially since he would have to shoot through Halloran. But his eyes were bleak as he sat, rigid, on the bed.

Westerman's mouth was open, and he perched so precariously on the edge of his chair that it looked as if he would fall off at any moment. Barrett had started back at the sight of the machine gun, and his face was white.

Partages alone looked unfazed by the threat of the situation.

"Damn you," he exploded violently, "so you're one of the murderers that killed Stackney! You—you—" His anger caused him to stutter helplessly.

The tall man swung the machine gun toward him and said in an even, dangerous voice, "Cut it, fat guy! You want a belly-ful of slugs?"

Barrett, who was close to Partages, put a hand on his shoulder. "Take it easy, Leon," he soothed. "Let's see what he wants."

Partages subsided, though he continued to glare viciously at the intruder.

The tall man smiled thinly. "That's better. Which one of you is Ed Race? That's the guy I'm after!"

Westerman, who was near the bed, started to point toward Ed.

Ed knew what was coming. The moment he was identified, a stream of slugs would pour into his body. They didn't intend to let him appear on the stage of the Clyde Theater that afternoon.

And so he acted now with the synchronized speed which his years of practice on the stage had developed to perfection. His right toe shot out, caught the rung of Westerman's chair, and pushed hard. Westerman, who had been sitting on the edge of his chair, went crashing to the floor, an expression of terrified surprise on his face.

THE TALL man's attention was deflected for an instant. And that instant was enough for Ed to send his heels high in the air, complete a somersault on the bed, and drop behind it at the far side.

The room rocked to the explosion of his heavy .45. The tall man was literally smashed backward against the door, the tommy-gun dropping from his hands. With a slug in his forehead, he was dead on his feet.

Ed heaved a sigh of relief as he climbed back over the bed. The shooting had been a little too close for comfort.

Barrett said sharply, "My God, Race, a man who can shoot like you is wasting his time on the stage!"

Westerman was scrambling to his feet, stammering, "M-my

g-glasses—they're b-broken." He picked up the empty rims of his spectacles, looked at them sorrowfully. "They cost ten dollars!"

Partages exclaimed, "To hell with your glasses!" Then he turned to Ed. "Look, Ed, this guy you just knocked off isn't the boss. They'll surely make another try at the theater. Are you still willing to go on with it?"

Ed smiled bleakly. He said softly, "You couldn't keep me away from it now, Mr. Partages. What time does the matinee show open?"

AT TWO-TWENTY-FIVE P.M. there was an air of tense expectancy about the Clyde Theater. Ed Race stood in the wings while the orchestra moved into the closing chords of the overture.

Several of the other actors waited there with him, among them Norma Maitland and the Peterman Brothers, who had appeared on many bills with Ed. Jerry Peterman, the small, sandy haired xylophonist, put a hand on Ed's sleeve and said very low, "Good luck, old man."

Ed nodded, thanking him with his eyes.

Westerman came up breathlessly, talking very loud so as to be heard above the crashing notes of the orchestra. "Everything is set, Mr. Race. The house is full of police. They'll be on the watch for the first suspicious movement in the audience. I myself will be up in the mezzanine box. I don't think there'll be a chance for anyone to get at you."

Ed grinned. "Anyway, I'll have half a chance." He tapped his chest, "Partages' bulletproof vest ought to give me some protection."

Norma Maitland, who was second on the bill after Ed, put her small hand on his arm and looked up into his face. Her eyes were wet. She could no longer restrain the tears. "Ed," she whispered in a husky, choked voice. "Be careful."

He patted her shoulder. "Don't get weepy, Norma. I'm hard to kill."

The little cardboard signs in the frames on either side of the stage slid down to reveal the sign: *The Masked Marksman.* The big dome light under the roof remained brilliantly lit as Ed adjusted the small mask over his face and stepped out onto the stage.

The tempo of the music changed. Ed bowed, straightened as the applause rose in volume, and walked to the table in the center of the stage on which four of his big revolvers were laid out. The other two were still in his shoulder holsters.

Beyond the table, at the other end of the stage, stood a tall wooden horse with twelve lighted candles.

Ed picked up three of the .45s, stepped to the footlights. The music ceased as he began to juggle. There was a strange stillness over the entire house. It was as if the audience sensed that there was something unusual about the situation—that death was in the air.

ED BOWED gracefully, his eyes scanning the audience. All he could make out was a sea of heads. He felt strangely calm, even in the thought that at any moment now, from somewhere in that packed house, might come a wicked *spat* and the whine of a bullet. Stackney had been shot through the heart. If he were attacked, would the assailant aim for the heart again? Or the attacker might assume that he had a bulletproof vest; in which case....

Even thoughts like these, however, failed to disturb the routine of his act. Once more he sent the three revolvers into the air, turning slightly to the left this time, to face the candles at the far end of the stage. The routine called for him to snuff those candles one after the other by firing the revolvers in rotation as they came down into his hands.

He was now facing toward the boxes, and looking up toward where Westerman had said he would be. The mezzanine box was empty.

About to complete his half turn toward the candles, his eye caught a slight motion of the curtain in that mezzanine box. The juggling of the three revolvers was child's play; he had often done it with his eyes closed. Now he watched that curtain keenly, delaying the moment when he would start firing at the candles. The orchestra leader was plainly nonplused. At this point the firing should have started.

But Ed's eyes were on those curtains at the rear of the box.

Slowly they parted and a small, black, ungainly looking object came into view. He stiffened as he recognized it for what it was—the silenced muzzle of a rifle.

It was trained directly at his head. Whoever was behind it no doubt knew about the bulletproof vest.

He caught one of the three revolvers as it came down into his hands, let the others fall to the floor, and went into a quick back somersault just as the weapon half hidden by the curtains up there bucked and *spatted*.

A slug whined across the stage and buried itself in the floor-boards.

Ed's somersault had saved him. He landed lithely on his feet, his heavy revolver rising with a sure, swift motion. The big .45 roared its deep-throated message of death just as a second shot was fired down at him.

Having kept his body constantly in motion, he was a difficult target. The second shot also missed him.

But his own went home. The curtains twisted as someone gripped them hard, and a body fell through into the box.

In motion at once, Ed leaped down into the orchestra pit, climbed over the low railing and raced over the stairway to the box.

The whole house was in pandemonium. Plainclothes men were arising from various seats, drawing revolvers, flourishing them, calling to people to be quiet. The orchestra played on discordantly, disconnectedly, the leader automatically waving his baton while his eyes followed Ed.

Ed was the first to reach the upper landing of the mezzanine floor. Behind him came Partages, who had been in the wings. Though fat, Partages was running fast; he had outdistanced the officer on guard alongside him.

Ed, making for the box, stumbled over an inert body on the floor. Not the man he had shot: he had seen that man fall into the box.

He stooped beside the body, Partages and the officer standing above him.

IT WAS Westerman. The theater manager stirred dazedly, opened his eyes. "Somebody—slugged me—before I got—in the box," he whispered.

Ed sprang up, leaped through the curtains. On the box floor, still gripping the silenced rifle, lay the bald-headed, stocky form of Charlie Barrett. He was dead. Ed's slug had fairly ripped away the left side of his face.

"My Gawd," Partages exclaimed, wheezing. "Charlie Barrett! Imagine—it was him all the time, trying to shake me down!"

Ed, bleak-eyed, turned away from the bloody spectacle, out of the enclosure.

"Hey," Partages demanded, "where are you goin'?"

Ed motioned toward the excited sea of faces below. "The show has to go on," he told Partages. "I'm going down and finish my number."

THE SPIDER

❏ #1: The Spider Strikes	$13.95
❏ #2: The Wheel of Death	$13.95
❏ #3: Wings of the Black Death	$13.95
❏ #4: City of Flaming Shadows	$13.95
❏ #5: Empire of Doom!	$13.95
❏ #6: Citadel of Hell	$13.95
❏ #7: The Serpent of Destruction	$13.95
❏ #8: The Mad Horde	$13.95
❏ #9: Satan's Death Blast	$13.95
❏ #10: The Corpse Cargo	$13.95
❏ #11: Prince of the Red Looters	$13.95
❏ #12: Reign of the Silver Terror	$13.95
❏ #13: Builders of the Dark Empire	$13.95
❏ #14: Death's Crimson Juggernaut	$13.95
❏ #15: The Red Death Rain	$13.95
❏ #16: The City Destroyer	$13.95
❏ #17: The Pain Emperor	$13.95
❏ #18: The Flame Master	$13.95
❏ #19: Slaves of the Crime Master	$13.95
❏ #20: Reign of the Death Fiddler	$13.95
❏ #21: Hordes of the Red Butcher	$13.95
❏ #22: Dragon Lord of the Underworld	$13.95
❏ #23: Master of the Death-Madness	$13.95
❏ #24: King of the Red Killers	$13.95
❏ #25: Overlord of the Damned	$13.95
❏ #26: Death Reign of the Vampire King	$13.95
❏ #27: Emperor of the Yellow Death	$13.95
❏ #28: The Mayor of Hell	$13.95
❏ #29: Slaves of the Murder Syndicate	$13.95
❏ #30: Green Globes of Death	$13.95
❏ #31: The Cholera King	$13.95
❏ #32: Slaves of the Dragon	$13.95
❏ #33: Legions of Madness	$12.95
❏ #34: Laboratory of the Damned	$12.95
❏ #35: Satan's Sightless Legion	$12.95
❏ #36: The Coming of the Terror	$12.95
❏ #37: The Devil's Death-Dwarfs	$12.95
❏ #38: City of Dreadful Night	$12.95
❏ #39: Reign of the Snake Men	$12.95
❏ #40: Dictator of the Damned	$12.95
❏ #41: The Mill-Town Massacres	$12.95
❏ #42: Satan's Workshop	$12.95
❏ #43: Scourge of the Yellow Fangs	$12.95
❏ #44: The Devil's Pawnbroker	$12.95
❏ #45: Voyage of the Coffin Ship	$12.95
❏ #46: The Man Who Ruled in Hell	$13.95
❏ #47: Slaves of the Black Monarch	$13.95
❏ #48: Machineguns Over the White House	$13.95
❏ #49: The City That Dared Not Eat	$13.95

❏ #50: Master of the Flaming Horde	$13.95
❏ #51: Satan's Switchboard	$13.95
❏ #52: Legions of the Accursed Light	$13.95
❏ #53: The City of Lost Men	$13.95
❏ #54: The Grey Horde Creeps	$13.95
❏ #55: City of Whispering Death	$13.95
❏ #56: When Thousands Slept in Hell	$13.95
❏ #57: Satan's Shakles	$14.95
❏ #58: The Emperor From Hell	$14.95
❏ #59: The Devil's Candlesticks	$14.95
❏ #60: The City That Paid to Die	$14.95
❏ #61: The Spider at Bay	$14.95
❏ #62: Scourge of the Black Legions	$14.95
❏ #63: The Withering Death	$14.95
❏ #64: Claws of the Golden Dragon	$14.95
❏ #65: The Song of Death	$14.95
❏ #66: The Silver Death Reign	$14.95
❏ #67: Blight of the Blazing Eye	$14.95
❏ #68: King of the Fleshless Legion	$14.95
❏ #69: Rule of the Monster Men	$16.95
❏ #70: The Spider and the Slaves of Hell	$16.95
❏ #71: The Spider and the Fire God	$16.95
❏ *NEW:* #72: The Corpse Broker	$16.95

THE WESTERN RAIDER

❏ #1: Guns of the Damned	$13.95
❏ #2: The Hawk Rides Back from Death	$13.95
❏ #3: Gun-Call for the Lost Legion	$13.95
❏ #4: The Law of Silver Trent	$13.95
❏ #5: The Gun-Prayer of Silver Trent	$13.95
❏ #6: Silver Trent Rides Alone	$13.95

G-8 AND HIS BATTLE ACES

❏ #1: The Bat Staffel	$13.95

CAPTAIN SATAN

❏ #1: The Mask of the Damned	$13.95
❏ #2: Parole for the Dead	$13.95
❏ #3: The Dead Man Express	$13.95
❏ #4: A Ghost Rides the Dawn	$13.95
❏ #5: The Ambassador From Hell	$13.95

DR. YEN SIN

❏ #1: Mystery of the Dragon's Shadow	$12.95
❏ #2: Mystery of the Golden Skull	$12.95
❏ #3: Mystery of the Singing Mummies	$12.95

RED FINGER

❏ #1: Second-Hand Death	$24.95

ACE G-MAN

- ❑ #1: The Suicide Squad Reports for Death $14.95
- ❑ #2: Coffins for the Suicide Squad $14.95
- ❑ #3: Shells for the Suicide Squad $14.95
- ❑ #4: The Suicide Squad in Corpse-Town $14.95
- ❑ #5: Wanted–In Three Pine Coffins $14.95
- ❑ #6: The Suicide Squad's Dawn Patrol $14.95
- ❑ #7: Targets for the Flaming Arrow $16.95

OPERATOR 5

- ❑ #1: The Masked Invasion $13.95
- ❑ #2: The Invisible Empire $13.95
- ❑ #3: The Yellow Scourge $13.95
- ❑ #4: The Melting Death $13.95
- ❑ #5: Cavern of the Damned $13.95
- ❑ #6: Master of Broken Men $13.95
- ❑ #7: Invasion of the Dark Legions $13.95
- ❑ #8: The Green Death Mists $13.95
- ❑ #9: Legions of Starvation $13.95
- ❑ #10: The Red Invader $13.95
- ❑ #11: The League of War-Monsters $13.95
- ❑ #12: The Army of the Dead $13.95
- ❑ #13: March of the Flame Marauders $13.95
- ❑ #14: Blood Reign of the Dictator $13.95
- ❑ #15: Invasion of the Yellow Warlords $13.95
- ❑ #16: Legions of the Death Master $13.95
- ❑ #17: Hosts of the Flaming Death $13.95
- ❑ #18: Invasion of the Crimson Death Cult $13.95
- ❑ #19: Attack of the Blizzard Men $13.95
- ❑ #20: Scourge of the Invisible Death $13.95
- ❑ #21: Raiders of the Red Death $13.95
- ❑ #22: War-Dogs of the Green Destroyer $13.95
- ❑ #23: Rockets From Hell $13.95
- ❑ #24: War-Masters from the Orient $13.95
- ❑ #25: Crime's Reign of Terror $13.95
- ❑ #26: Death's Ragged Army $13.95
- ❑ #27: Patriots' Death Battalion $13.95
- ❑ #28: The Bloody Forty-five Days $13.95
- ❑ #29: America's Plague Battalions $13.95
- ❑ #30: Liberty's Suicide Legions $13.95
- ❑ #31: Siege of the Thousand Patriots $13.95
- ❑ #32: Patriots' Death March $14.95
- ❑ #33: Revolt of the Lost Legions $14.95
- ❑ #34: Drums of Destruction $14.95
- ❑ #35: The Army Without a Country $14.95
- ❑ #36: The Bloody Frontiers $14.95
- ❑ #37: The Coming of the Mongol Hordes $14.95
- ❑ #38: The Siege That Brought Black Death $16.95
- ❑ #39: Revolt of the Devil Men $16.95

THE MASKED MARKSMAN

- ❑ *NEW:* #1: Death Takes an Encore $16.95

CAPTAIN COMBAT

- ❑ #1: The Sky Beast of Berlin $13.95
- ❑ #2: Red Wings For the Blood Battalion $13.95
- ❑ #3: Low Ceiling For Nazi Hell Hawks $13.95

DUSTY AYRES AND HIS BATTLE BIRDS

- ❑ #1: Black Lightning! $13.95
- ❑ #2: Crimson Doom $13.95
- ❑ #3: The Purple Tornado $13.95
- ❑ #4: The Screaming Eye $13.95
- ❑ #5: The Green Thunderbolt $13.95
- ❑ #6: The Red Destroyer $13.95
- ❑ #7: The White Death $13.95
- ❑ #8: The Black Avenger $13.95
- ❑ #9: The Silver Typhoon $13.95
- ❑ #10: The Troposphere F-S $13.95
- ❑ #11: The Blue Cyclone $13.95
- ❑ #12: The Tesla Raiders $13.95

MAVERICKS

- ❑ #1: Five Against the Law $12.95
- ❑ #2: Mesquite Manhunters $12.95
- ❑ #3: Bait for the Lobo Pack $12.95
- ❑ #4: Doc Grimson's Outlaw Posse $12.95
- ❑ #5: Charlie Parr's Gunsmoke Cure $12.95

THE MYSTERIOUS WU FANG

- ❑ #1: The Case of the Six Coffins $12.95
- ❑ #2: The Case of the Scarlet Feather $12.95
- ❑ #3: The Case of the Yellow Mask $12.95
- ❑ #4: The Case of the Suicide Tomb $12.95
- ❑ #5: The Case of the Green Death $12.95
- ❑ #6: The Case of the Black Lotus $12.95
- ❑ #7: The Case of the Hidden Scourge $12.95

THE SECRET 6

- ❑ #1: The Red Shadow $13.95
- ❑ #2: House of Walking Corpses $13.95
- ❑ #3: The Monster Murders $13.95
- ❑ #4: The Golden Alligator $13.95

CAPTAIN ZERO

- ❑ #1: City of Deadly Sleep $13.95
- ❑ #2: The Mark of Zero! $13.95
- ❑ #3: The Golden Murder Syndicate $13.95